HERBERT'S WORMHOLE

AEROSTAR AND THE
3½- POINT PLAN OF VENGEANCE

HERBIE WORM

AEROSTAR AND THE 3½-

Peter Nelson

ERT'S
HOLE

POINT PLAN OF VENGEANCE

Rohitash Rao

HARPER
An Imprint of HarperCollinsPublishers

For Diane, the light, love,
and lunch lady of my life. —P.N.

This is for my nephew, Jadon Dinesh Rao.
I love you, but seriously, put down the iPad. —R.R.

Herbert's Wormhole: AeroStar and the 3 1/2-Point Plan of Vengeance

Copyright © 2013 by Peter Nelson and Rohitash Rao
www.harpercollinschildrens.com

ISBN 978-0-06-201220-3

Typography by Alison Klapthor

13 14 15 16 17 CG/RRDH 10 9 8 7 6 5 4 3 2 1

First Edition

Alex Filby walked into the living room to find his little sister, Ellie, aiming a blaster at the television.

"*Watch me, Alexth!*" she demanded—with a lisp. "I'M GONNA BLOW THITH THLIME-THUCKING FREAK INTO A GATHILLION THPATHE-CHUNKTH!"

Not only did this strike Alex as oddly familiar, it also struck him as odd. Especially since the television wasn't turned on. Even if it had been, his mom had dismantled the AlienSlayer video game console and filled its insides with MightyGlue.

He grabbed the video game blaster out of his

five-year-old sister's hand. "Ellie, knock it off. You're gonna make us miss the school bus. Besides, you know Mom doesn't want you even *pretending* to play video games."

"You're jutht jealouth—becauth I'm *vithual*."

She meant *visual*, and all *that* meant was she had a vivid imagination. *Big deal*, Alex thought. What little kid didn't? So she had about seven hundred fifty or so stuffed animals and had given each one its own name. And its own nickname. And favorite color, family history, food allergies, and shoe size (for the ones with feet). Okay, so Alex had to admit she had an impressive imagination. But *jealouth*—er, *jealous*? Please. He mainly thought she was annoying. And spoiled. Oh, and super bossy.

"*MOM! ALEXTH HATHN'T MADE ME MY THINNAMON RAITHIN TOATHT!*"

"*What?* You never asked me to make you cinnamon rais—"

"Alex, *please!*" Mrs. Filby rushed in, buttoning up her best gardening smock. "I asked you to help get your sister breakfast and see that she's ready for school! Why is she watching television? You're going to make her late for the bus!"

"*Mom, I—*"

"Alex, you know I have an important Merwinsville United League of Community Harvesters meeting this morning. I need you to get your sister ready!"

Alex's mom was the president of M.U.L.C.H., the local community gardening group. They were a bunch of ladies who basically just grew flowers and vegetables in the community gardens down at Merwinsville Public Park. And in Alex's opinion, they had way more meetings than they really needed.

"Mom, Ellie can get her own cinnamon raisin toast."

"No, Alex, she can't. She's only four."

"I'm five!"

Mrs. Filby beamed at Ellie. "Almost, my little *rutabaga!* Not till Saturday!"

Alex rolled his eyes and headed for the kitchen. Until very recently, Alex's mom used to call him sappy, embarrassing names. That was when she'd thought he spent his time playing spaceman with his friends. Since he quit that and was now going into sixth grade, his mom had decided to stop giving him nicknames like her *babushka* and start giving him responsibilities like taking care of his sister. It wasn't easy—there were times when he missed being called a babushka.

He also didn't need reminding that his sister's birthday was this Saturday. It was all everyone in the house had been talking about for weeks.

"Hey, sport! Excited about your sister's big birthday this weekend?"

Alex's dad was sitting over a cup of coffee and smiling down at a toy catalog.

"Uh, yeah. Sure."

"I've got a big surprise being delivered for Ellie Saturday morning. Wanna help me assemble it? I'll let you use my monkey wrench again."

Before Alex could think of a way to say no, Mr. Filby suddenly jumped up and wiped his mouth. "Oh! Look at the time! I'm late for my M.E.G.A. meeting! Gotta blast off!"

Until very recently, Alex's dad had been into alien-blasting video games. *Way* into them. His mom had decided enough was enough, dismantled the game, and sent Mr. Filby to a class to help people overcome the urge to blast aliens on their televisions. Alex's dad came back a changed man with a new outlook on otherworldly visitors. He also came back a member of the Merwinsville Extraterrestrial Greeters Association, a group of grown-ups who not only believed there were other forms of life in the galaxy, but that they could show up any day and would need someone to welcome them and show them around town.

"If I'm late to the meeting, they'll assume I was abducted again!"

Alex's parents were weird.

The funny thing about his dad being a member of M.E.G.A. was that Alex could have told him his club was totally right about the existence of aliens. He also could've told them when they'd show up (in about fifty years), what they looked like (large, blobby, squidlike creatures with fake wigs and mustaches), and what they were called (G'Daliens, because they spoke with nonthreatening Australian accents and tended to say nonthreatening Australian-type things like "G'Day!").

Alex had met G'Daliens. Real, live ones. Lots of them. He and his next-door neighbors Herbert Slewg and Sammi Clementine were in fact quite well-known by the entire G'Dalien race. You might even say they were famous.

G'DALIENS

All through last summer, Alex, Herbert, and Sammi had enjoyed access to a wormhole that connected them to the future. Specifically, to their little town of Merwinsville *one hundred years* in the future. The wormhole was located inside the tube slide on Alex's backyard jungle gym. Herbert had invented what he called Negative Energy Densifyer suits, which enabled the wearers to activate the wormhole as well as pass through it.

LAST SUMMER

TIME TO GO THROUGH THE WORMHOLE! I'LL GO FIRST.

Without a working N.E.D. suit, both the wormhole and the future world it connected to would be hidden and sealed off forever.

Which is kind of exactly what had happened. At the end of the summer, Alex, Herbert, and Sammi had decided the responsible thing to do was to stop messing around with time travel. They said good-bye to the future, returned to the present, and sent the suits through the wormhole to be destroyed, closing the wormhole forever.

Alex stopped buttering his sister's cinnamon-raisin toast and looked up.

The future was awesome. It was filled with not just G'Daliens, who were friendly, but all the amazing stuff they gave to future earthlings—the kind of stuff any member of M.E.G.A., M.U.L.C.H., or the entire human race would've found very helpful. And in the future, Alex, Herbert, and Sammi had been superheroes, because everyone there thought they'd defeated a different race of decidedly unfriendly aliens. They hadn't, but everyone *thought* they had, which made them known and loved by just about everyone. And it was, well, awesome.

But now Alex could never go to future Merwinsville again. Worse, *he couldn't even talk about it.* This was because he, Herbert, and Sammi had agreed to what Herbert called a "sacred vow of solemn silence." This meant that not only had they shut themselves off from the future, but they had to shut their mouths about it, too. And as a former ultra-famous, beloved, superhero AlienSlayer who, until very recently, lived for dangerous adventures and loved bragging about it, this sacred vow of solemn silence was really beginning to bug the sacred crud out of Alex.

"ALEXTH! WHERE'TH MY THINNAMON RAITHIN TOATHT?"

"Alex, please hurry. Your sister's hungry." Alex's mom rushed into the kitchen, adjusting her gardening hat, the one with the red ladybugs printed on it. She kissed Alex on top of the head. "See that she's not late for school. They're throwing her a birthday party in class today! Isn't that exciting?"

"Yeah," Alex said, flicking a raisin off his thumb.

"WAIT! WAIT! HOLD THE BUS! HOLD UP!"

Visions of futuristic, G'Dalien-designed pneumatic pedestrian transporters, vapor-fueled jetpacks, and antigravity basketball sneakers rushed through Alex's brain as he huffed and puffed to catch the bus, which was about to pull away. *SCRREECH!* It came to a stop, and the doors opened with a *whoosh.* Alex grabbed the railing and bent over to catch his breath. "*Sorry,*" he said, panting to the bus driver. "*Little sister . . . had to say good-bye . . . to all of her . . . stupid stuffed animals.*" He looked back at Ellie strolling down the sidewalk, holding her best stuffed teddy bear, head held high, with a proud grin on her puffy little face.

She stepped over her winded brother. "I *told* you they wouldn't leave without the birthday *printheth.*"

Alex walked toward an empty seat near the back of the bus. Amid the sea of heads, he immediately noticed one wearing a strange-looking helmet with wires, computer chips, and antennae sticking out of it, as well as a black glass visor in front, hiding the face of the kid who was wearing it. Alex knew exactly whose face was in there.

Alex sneered at his neighbor. "New invention, *genius?*"

Herbert pulled the helmet off his head, which made his hair stand up even funnier than usual. Ignoring Alex, he set the helmet in his lap, adjusted his glasses, and began making tiny adjustments to its tiny electronic panel with a tiny screwdriver.

"Don't even try," said a girl's voice behind him. "He's in a mood."

Alex turned around to see Sammi Clementine smiling at him.

"Well, that makes two of us," he said.

"Not *this* again," Sammi said. "Just give it up, already."

"Exactly! That's what drives me crazy! *Why'd we give it up?*"

"Because. It could cause problems, in our time or in"—she lowered her voice—"*the other one*. So we gave it up. That's what we decided."

"That's what *he* decided." Alex nodded to Herbert, who was furiously tinkering with his weird helmet, getting more frustrated by the second. "I honestly don't know why we agreed to it. I was a superhero! I went on awesome adventures with my 111-year-old self! Who happens to be awesome! I was half of a butt-kicking, alien-slaying, city-saving superduo!

Here I'm just a boring kid making boring cinnamon raisin toast in a boring town—totally bored!" He stopped ranting and squinted at Sammi. "C'mon. Admit it. *So are you.*"

Sammi stared back at him. Of course she missed the fun of traveling to the future, the adventure, and especially all the wonderful friends she'd met there.

"Sure, life's not quite as exciting as it was, but I guess I just feel—"

"She *feels*—" Herbert spoke from beside them, his eyes staring sternly at Alex. "She feels what I *know*. That the potential for disaster in what we were doing was too great. Destroying the suits was the only logical thing to do. Hence our sacred vow of solemn silence."

"Look who's eggheaded his way into the conversation," Alex snapped back at him. "Why don't you take a break from working on your electro bike helmet there and whip us up a few new N.E.D. suits so we can be future-heroes again, *Brain-Boy*?"

"You don't think I want to sometimes? You don't think I miss the incredible technological advances and inventions we saw? You don't think

I'm bored with *my* inventions? Look, I 'invented' you something, for your disgusting hot dogs-onna-stick."

Herbert riffled through his oversize backpack, pulled out a small remote control toy tank and placed it on the bus floor. Alex leaned down to watch as Herbert used the remote to drive it toward him. Its cannon slowly raised, took aim at Alex and— *SPLORT!* The cannon shot out a spurge of bright orangey-colored cheese right in Alex's face.

"*Aaauuugggh!*" Alex fell backward in his seat as Herbert quickly picked up his invention and stuffed it back in his pack.

"See? Even my Goopy-Cheeze Battle Blaster doesn't work properly. The calibration is—"

"*SLEWWWG!*" Alex's goop-covered face was suddenly diving toward Herbert. He tackled him into the aisle as the other kids cheered on the fight.

Sammi sat back in her seat and finished her thought to no one. "What I was going to say was I *feel* that at least the three of us became friends." She sighed sadly.

Twenty minutes later, Herbert and Alex stepped out of the principal's office to find Sammi waiting for them on a bench in the hallway.

"They gave us a warning, but they confiscated his Goopy-Cheeze Battle thingy." Alex shrugged.

"For what it's worth, I thought it was pretty cool," Sammi said.

"*Phh,*" Herbert spat angrily. "All I do is repurpose toys and household objects into slightly dangerous—"

"Or *annoying*—" Alex added.

"—pseudo-inventions. I can't make things like the G'Daliens. I'm no inventor."

"Dude, you invented the greatest invention ever invented!" Alex said. "You came up with the N.E.D. suits that allowed us to pass through the wormhole! All you gotta do is whip up a few more of those suckers, and we're back in business! You get to hang out with your Old Man self and drool all over the G'Dalien gadgets, I get to reunite with my Old Man self and have adventures, and Sammi—"

Alex stopped. He and Herbert both looked at Sammi, remembering that she never got to meet her future self. "It's okay." She shrugged. "I never really wanted to meet my 111-year-old self. It seems to me that turning into a grown-up is weird enough without knowing the parallel universe version of who I might turn out to be."

"It doesn't matter," Herbert suddenly snapped. "We agreed. The power to travel through that wormhole created a potentially cataclysmic threat to the balance of the time/space continuum. *Especially if it ever fell into the wrong hands.*"

"Right. Like GOR-DON was going to squeeze his blobby butt into that little suit and pay a visit to your *mom.*"

GOR-DON was a particularly mean and nasty G'Dalien they'd had the unpleasant experience of making their enemy in the future. Having him show up in the present would *not* be a good thing. And he did have quite the blobby butt.

"Again, it doesn't matter," Herbert repeated. "We all agreed that it's over and that we'd stop talking about it. So we're going to stop talking about it . . . *NOW.*"

"Why? Because of your stupid silent vowel of silence?"

"It was a *sacred vow of solemn silence.* And yes, precisely."

"Ugh. I swear, if I hear you say that one more time . . ."

"I shouldn't have to say it at all, you adventure-seeking dimwit! That's the whole point of it being silent! You don't bring it up, you don't change it, and you *can't undo it*! *AND THAT'S WHAT MAKES IT SOLEMN—GET IT?*"

A few students looked over at them. Herbert, red-faced, quieted himself.

"Guys, let's just drop it," Sammi said. "The important thing is we got to share this cool adventure together and now we're friends."

"*Please*," Herbert said. "Like I have *anything* in common with this superhero wannabe."

Alex's eyes narrowed at this. "Or this genius inventor never-was."

"What are you guys saying?" Sammi asked. "So you're not friends?"

Alex glanced at Herbert. "No, we're not. Friends don't make friends take sacred solemn vows that are *seriously stupid.*"

"*Stupid?*" Herbert was seething again. "Did you say *stupid?*"

"Yes!" Alex stepped forward so he was nearly nose-to-nose with Herbert. "Stupid because we stupidly promised that we'd never talk about, mention, or even hint at the *fact* that the three of us were—"

He stopped himself. Herbert glared at him. Sammi quietly shook her head no. Alex looked over at the crowd of students then back at Herbert. He took a deep breath and suddenly bellowed to everyone in the hallway:

THE THREE OF US WERE SUPERHERO ALIENSLAYERS WHO TRAVELED THROUGH THE WORMHOLE A HUNDRED YEARS INTO THE FUTURE, WHERE WE FOUGHT ALIENS AND SAVED THE WHOLE WORLD, AND POSSIBLY THE ENTIRE GALAXY—TWICE!!!

There was a heavy silence. Herbert and Sammi stared wide-eyed at each other. Even Alex couldn't believe what he had just done. They all turned slowly to face the students. Everyone was staring at them.

"Check it out, you guys!" A burly kid, Moose Herrington, suddenly shouted. "Filby's even better at making up imaginary friends than his baby sister!"

The entire lobby burst out laughing. Adriana Catalina, a long-haired sixth grade girl, chimed in. "Gee, Sammi! So *that's* why you dropped out of dance class—to travel to the future and fight aliens with your two *boyfriends*!"

The kids walked off laughing, leaving Alex, Herbert, and Sammi standing shell-shocked for a moment. Herbert turned to them.

"I was *wrong*," he said to a stunned Alex and Sammi, who had never heard this phrase fall out of the mouth of Herbert Slewg. "Apparently, Alex, you *can* disregard our sacred vow of solemn silence. I should've theorized that no one would believe a babbling idiot like you anyway."

"*Herbert!*" Sammi gasped.

Ignoring her, he pulled his helmet out of his backpack, put it on his head, and turned to walk away.

"*SLEWWWWWG!*" In an instant, Alex was on top of him. Herbert's helmeted head hit the floor with a loud *CLUNK!* Sammi raced to pull the two of them apart as they continued to yell terrible names in each other's faces.

"*Eggheaded, science-loving, nerdy know-it-all!*"

"*Brainless, boneheaded, thrill-seeking simpleton!*"

In the struggle, Sammi suddenly fell backward, slamming loudly into a locker with a *CRASH!* She slumped to the floor and began to cry. Alex and Herbert stopped immediately and rushed to her. She pushed them away and stumbled to her feet.

"*Get away from me, both of you!*" Sammi said.

"I'm tired of your stupid fighting. I'm tired of both of you! You're right—one of you loves science and technology, the other loves adventure and being a hero. But you're forgetting that you *had* two things in common—that wormhole and *me* as a friend! We gave away one, and you just lost the other. So go ahead and hate each other now. Just leave me out of it, *and leave me alone.*"

Sammi gathered her backpack from the floor and ran down the hall. Alex and Herbert looked at each other with mouths hanging open. Neither knew what to say. A horn caught their attention, and they looked up to see a parade of kindergartners pass carrying a large golden Birthday Throne complete with balloons, glitter, and streamers. Sitting atop it was Ellie, wearing a sparkly birthday crown, looking like a very tiny but very bossy Queen of Egypt.

"Perfect," Alex said to himself. "Just perfect."

CHAPTER 3

"All right, you slime-sucking freak! Get ready to be blown into a gazillion space-chunks, courtesy of Alex Filby—the greatest AlienSlayer in all the known universe!"

Alex crouched fiercely in his best tiger-warrior pose, bravely wearing his super-flexible El Solo Libre uniform: tighty-whities stretched over his N.E.D. suit, flowing cape, and Mexican wrestler mask. He leered up at a gigantic Six-Clawed Corinthian Space Crab. It stood thirty feet tall on its tiny hind legs and snapped its giant razor-sharp claws in the air. *SHIK! SHIK-SHIK!* Alex smirked as he narrowed his gaze at the crusty-shelled creature. Then suddenly he leaped—soaring straight at its armored midsection.

WUMP!

Alex bounced off and fell backward. The Space Crab advanced, snipping the air with crabby glee. *CRUNCH!* One of its claws came smashing down, just missing Alex as he rolled out of the way. *CRUNCH! CRUNCH!* Two more claws narrowly missed him as he tried to scramble to his feet. *CRUNCH!* An open claw crashed down, pinning Alex to the ground. The giant space-crustacean let out a delighted *squeeeal!* It raised a boulder-size claw twelve feet above Alex's head. Helplessly held in place, Alex shut his eyes as the claw drew back and—

CRUNCH!

"*Aaaah!*" Alex sat up in his bed. He looked around his bedroom, then checked to make sure his head wasn't a mushy stump. *Whew!* It had been a nightmare. Or rather, a morningmare, seeing as the sun was streaming through his window.

CRUNCH!

Alex jumped out of bed, ran to the window, and looked into his backyard. *CRUNCH!* Alex saw his dad seated in a small tractorlike machine. Printed on the side of it was WRENT-A-WRECKING-BALL. His dad pulled a lever and the crane swung back a giant steel ball. He pushed the lever and it swung again—*CRUNCH!* The ball slammed into Alex's jungle gym, smashing the tube slide into giant pieces.

"Noooooooooo!" Alex screamed all the way down the stairs, through the kitchen, onto the back porch, down the steps, and into the backyard. He couldn't believe his eyes. His jungle gym was demolished—just a big heap of scrap.

"Oh, hey, Big Guy!" His father waved to him excitedly from the cockpit of the Wrent-A-Wrecking-Ball. "Change your mind about helping me with your sister's surprise?" Dumbfounded, Alex looked to see a giant box near the back of the house. Printed on it in bright pink and purple was *Fluffy Stuff 'n' Pals Teaparty Townhouse (SOME SERIOUS ASSEMBLY REQUIRED)*.

Alex bent and picked up a chunk of what used to be his tube slide.

"I know you outgrew that old jungle gym," his father said over the rumble of the idling wrecker. "Never see you and your friends play on it like you used to. Well, you had some fun times out here—now it's your sister's turn. Right, Champ?"

Alex didn't answer. He turned from the heap that used to be his wormhole, trudged into the yard next door—and stepped straight up to Herbert's front door.

Ding-dong-VROOM! Staring ahead, Alex automatically ducked as a small vacuum hose with a fake nose-and-mustache sprang out of a small panel beside the Slewgs' front door. The DoorSmell—just another one of Herbert's stupid inventions. It missed Alex and snapped back into its compartment. Mrs. Slewg opened the door.

"Alex! How nice to sniff you!" she chirped. Alex nodded and headed up.

Ignoring the KEEP OUT signs plastered on Herbert's door, Alex entered. Providing Herbert with a place to sleep was not the primary function of this bedroom. Herbert used it as a lab—a place to work on his inventions, conduct scientific experiments, and figure out elaborate mathematical equations. He had a bed, of course, but it was used for sleeping only when absolutely necessary. To find Herbert standing in the center of his room wearing his weird electronic helmet wasn't actually a strange occurrence. Alex watched him yank it off in frustration and go to pick up his tiny tool kit to make an adjustment. Then he realized he wasn't alone.

"*Ahh!*" he squealed, startled. "What are you doing here?"

"I know we're not friends or anything, but in case you were thinking of making a new N.E.D. suit, don't bother. It's over. It's really, finally, completely over."

He nodded toward the window. Herbert set down his helmet, walked across his cluttered room, and looked out at Alex's backyard. He watched as Alex's dad swung his Wrent-A-Wrecking-Ball too aggressively, accidentally demolishing the Filbys' built-in barbecue.

"Great," Herbert said. "Now I'll never figure out how to get this to work." He crossed back and picked up the helmet. "Just another failed invention."

"What are you talking about?" Alex asked. "What is that thing, anyway?"

Herbert looked at him. "It's supposed to be a Parallel Universe Perspective Enhancer. I began working on it as a concept with Old Man Me before we left the future. I built it here but can't get it to function correctly. I can't—I'm not . . . *smart enough.*"

Alex looked at him. He'd never seen Herbert Slewg look so defeated. "So you wanted to go through the wormhole again, too, to figure out how to get your hat to work! Why didn't you do it? Why didn't you just make another N.E.D. suit, go through, and figure it out?"

Herbert tossed the helmet on his bed, crossed to his closet, and opened it. Hanging there were at least a dozen silver suits. On the floor were even

more, crumpled and discarded like some sort of aluminum laundry pile. He scooped them all up and stormed to his window.

"I tried, *okay*? I was just lucky the first time. Turns out, I'm not even smart enough to reinvent something I invented. This was all just a waste of time!" He dumped the silver suits into a bin marked *FAILED INVENTIONS*. Alex looked out the window and saw that the bin emptied through the wall into a large Dumpster below.

Alex turned back to see Herbert sitting on his bed, his head in his hands. He walked over to him, picked up the helmet, put it on, and slid down the dark glass visor. "So what's it supposed to do?" His voice was muffled from inside the helmet.

"My 111-year-old self had begun developing some theories about alternate parallel versions of the same person. He sensed a kind of telepathic link between himself and me even before we physically met. Once we did meet, our parallel paths overlapped, and together we began testing his theories in the SlayerLair lab. We isolated a synaptic cerebral signal and eventually designed a transmitter that could harness and transmit that signal in the form of mental images between the two parallel versions of the same person—from opposite ends of the wormhole."

Alex took off the helmet and blinked. "Hi. I'm Alex. I speak English."

Herbert took the helmet from him and sighed. "*If* I were a good inventor and could get mine to work, I'd be able to put it on and communicate with Old Man Me while he wore *his*. I would see my world through the visor but also get a fuzzy glimpse of what he's looking at, on a smaller holo-screen. And vice versa. He sees what I see, an entire century and alternate universe away."

"Kinda like a video wormhole walkie-talkie dealio. *Cool*."

"Er, *kinda*. I've got the components right but can't figure out the proper connection schematics to get it to work. And now"—he looked out the window at the rubble that was once the tube slide, jungle gym, and their personal wormhole—"I'll never be able to ask the one person who could've taught me how to finish building my Parallel Universe Perspective Enhancer."

Alex stepped up beside him. "I know this is probably a bad time to point this out, but you do realize those letters spell *P.U.P.E.*, right?"

Alex approached his back deck steps and handed a still-sulky Herbert an inappropriately large wedge of birthday cake. Herbert set down his P.U.P.E. helmet and accepted the cake. Alex sat down, and the two of them stared out at an enormous hulking object covered in a giant sheet in the center of his backyard. Flitting around it like crazed, wingless MoonBats were a swarm of about fifty kindergarten girls.

Even though the birthday party was winding down, Alex didn't know how much more of this he could take.

"So, is that what's left of it, under there?" Herbert nodded glumly toward the giant sheet.

"No," Alex said. "My dad had the jungle gym hauled off to the recycling dump. It's gone. That's my sister's birthday present."

"Oh."

"All *right, everyone!*" Mrs. Filby suddenly trumpeted. "Gather round! It's time for the grand unveiling!" The kids were corralled in a circle around the massive covered object. Mr. Filby stepped up and led the crowd in a rousing countdown.

"*FIVE! FOUR! THREE! TWO! ONE! HAPPY BIRTHDAY, ELLIE!*" He pulled off the cover to reveal the *Fluffy Stuff 'n' Pals Teaparty Townhouse*. It was a hideous purple and pink, all-plastic, two-story structure the size of a tall, narrow cottage.

"Eeeeeeeeeeeee!" The girls let out an ear-splitting scream and gathered around Ellie as she went to open the thick, plastic front door. It didn't budge. She tried again but still nothing. The other girls instinctively backed away from her as her cheeks began to redden and her tiny fists began to tremble.

"DADDY!"

Mr. Filby rushed up, assuring everyone not to panic. He looked over at Herbert for scientific reinforcement as he babbled something about molecules expanding in the sun.

"Just—*open it, Darryl,*" Mrs. Filby interjected.

Mr. Filby rolled up his sleeves, grabbed the oversize plastic doorknob, and tugged at the door. It seemed to be locked from the inside. He walked around the town house and observed that the windows on both floors were shut and locked, as well. He looked over at Alex. "Hey, Sport. You two wanna give me a hand?"

"Why don't you just knock it down with your Wrent-A-Wrecking-Ball?" Alex muttered under his breath. He and Herbert grabbed the cartoonishly large doorknob and, with his father, tugged with all their might—but couldn't open it.

"This is the worst birthday, *ever!*" Ellie ran inside the Filby house, pretty much bringing the party to an awkward end. Mrs. Filby ran after her, babbling something about getting the town house fixed in the morning and filling it with brand-new stuffed animals.

The sun was beginning to set, so Mr. Filby thanked all of Ellie's guests, doled out goody-bags, and sent everyone on their way. Then he plopped on the couch, turned on the Unexplained Phenomena Channel, and didn't move for the rest of the evening.

Alex and Herbert sat alone outside, staring up at the ugly little playhouse.

"I guess it's officially official," Alex said. "We're retired."

"I'll never see my 111-year-old self again—or all that amazing G'Dalien technology."

"I'll never see my 111-year-old self or have another amazing adventure. I'll miss Old Man Alex. He really got me."

"Technically, he really *was* you." Herbert grabbed his helmet and stood up. He gave one last look at the ugly, plastic, mega dollhouse and tossed his pink paper plate into a trash can. "Thanks for the cake," he said. "I'll see you around." Then he walked back toward his house, dropping his P.U.P.E. helmet in the Failed Inventions bin.

Alex turned to go inside but stopped to get one last look at Ellie's new *Fluffy Stuff 'n' Pals Teaparty Townhouse.* He stepped onto the grass, placed his hand on the knob, and slowly turned it. The door was still locked shut.

He noticed something out of the corner of his eye and saw a black head of hair just visible over his backyard fence, which separated his house from Sammi's. She peeked over the fence, spotted him looking at her, and disappeared again.

"Sammi!" Alex ran to the fence. It was too tall for him to climb, so he spoke into the wood. "Sammi, are you there?"

"What do you want?" her voice said flatly.

"I'm sorry. You were right. We were being jerks." He waited, listening, wondering if she was still there. "The wormhole's gone. My dad tore it down."

"I know."

"But Herbert and I, we— Well, I don't want to say we're *great friends* or anything. But we both just had cake together. So that's something."

"It's none of my business," her voice said, with what Alex thought was a trace of sadness. "Goodbye, Alex."

Alex knew Sammi had left, but he stood there for a long while anyway. "Bye, Sammi," he said to himself. He turned and looked at the towering plastic structure that now dominated his backyard. "And bye, wormhole." He thought how Herbert would at least sleep better knowing it could never fall into the wrong hands. Feeling lonely and sad, he still smiled a tiny smile as he pictured GOR-DON's blobby butt stuffed into a tiny little silver N.E.D. suit.

Alex woke with a start and sat up in bed. It was the middle of the night.

SLAM!

He rushed to his window and looked down on the tea party town house, just visible in the darkness.

SLAM! The sound was coming from the tea party town house.

Alex crept downstairs and into the backyard. He could feel his heart pounding in his throat and a slight breeze in his hair. He crept up to the town house doorknob and reached out his hand very slowly. . . . The door suddenly flew open. *"Aaaah!"* Alex stumbled backward onto the ground.

Terrified, he peered into the dark town house. No one was there. The door stood wide open, until another breeze blew the door shut. *SLAM!*

Relieved and a little embarrassed, Alex exhaled and looked up at the sky. The moon was a half-full, smiling slab of white, completely dark on one side. He smiled back at it, imagining how his friend Old Man Alex would laugh at him for being so spooked by an oversize dollhouse. After a while, he got up and went back to bed.

The next morning, Alex buttered his sister's cinnamon-raisin toast. "C'mon, Ellie! We're gonna be late for the bus again!" She came marching down the stairs with an armful of stuffed animals—her third trip that morning, relocating her friends into the *Fluffy Stuff 'n' Pals Teaparty Townhouse*. In the light

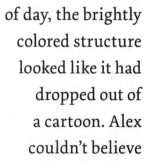

of day, the brightly colored structure looked like it had dropped out of a cartoon. Alex couldn't believe

it had scared him. Ellie dumped the animals somewhere inside it, then alerted some imaginary friend of her morning routine. "I've gotta eat breakfatht, then I'll be right back!"

Alex's mom and dad were arguing in the kitchen. "Oh, *of course*, dear," his mom said, sounding a little like a sarcastic computer Alex once knew. "I'm *sure* aliens come to our town *all the time*, just to visit the community gardens."

"The proof is undeniable!" Mr. Filby shouted back. He was waving a photocopied flyer in her face. "All M.E.G.A. wants is a soil sample—the truth is in there, and I think it's a bit more important to this community than your *radishes*!"

"Radishes were *last season*," Mrs. Filby shot back.

She quickly kissed Alex and Ellie on top of their heads. "I'm off. Emergency M.U.L.C.H. meeting at the park."

"Well, I'm off, too!" Mr. Filby countered, and he kissed Alex and Ellie even quicker. "Emergency *M.E.G.A. meeting* at the park!" They both gave each other a look, then suddenly raced out the door, jumped into their separate cars, and squealed out of the driveway.

"C'mon, Ellie." Alex sighed. "Time to catch the bus."

"Okay. Let me thay good-bye to Mithter Blobby Panth."

Alex waited patiently from the back porch, listening to Ellie yelling up the spiral staircase of her town house. "Bye, Mithter Blobby Panth! Take care of my friendth till I get home! And don't forget, no dairy in Uncle Bunny'th tea—or he'll get gathy!" Alex rolled his eyes as she shut the town house door and ran past him.

On the bus, Alex gave a nod to Herbert as he passed, and spotted Sammi sitting all alone. As he approached, she put her backpack on the empty side of the seat and continued staring straight ahead.

Alex moved on and sat next to a second grader with a runny nose.

The three former AlienSlayers walked into school separately but were struck by a common realization as they remembered the ridicule of the day before. Expecting more taunting, they instead saw everyone in the school crowded around the bulletin board. Alex and Herbert pushed through the crowd and saw, tacked on the center of the board, the same flyer that Alex's dad had waved in his mom's face.

M.E.G.A.
COMMUNITY ALERT

Merwinsville Extraterrestrial Greeters Association Community Alert: This photo of an extraterrestrial was taken in the Merwinsville Community Gardens Saturday night. Be on the lookout for any alien beings, species, or creatures.

If seen, please remember to be friendly and welcoming, then immediately contact your neighborhood M.E.G.A. member or

CALL THE ALIEN HOTLINE:
1-800-HEY-MEGA

Alex and Herbert glanced at each other. "No way," Alex said first. "There's no way. Right?" Herbert stepped closer to get a better look at the picture.

"Oh, thank goodness! We're saved!" Moose Herrington's voice boomed loudly, as usual. "Our very own time-traveling alien slayers are here!" The crowd started laughing. "Oh, no!" Adriana Catalina said. "Where's the third member of your little spaceman club?"

Alex and Herbert pushed back out through the crowd as Adriana continued.

"Did Sammi finally realize what a couple of nerdy losers you are?" The two of them ignored the laughter, quickly exiting the crowd. They stopped short when they spotted Sammi watching the scene by her locker. She quickly shut it and walked down the hall.

"It's utterly inconceivable," Herbert said. He and Alex were sitting in the cafeteria, trying to ignore the laughs and chuckles they were getting from most of their classmates.

Alex was getting very excited. "Dude, you saw the picture!"

"We shouldn't jump to any conclusions," Herbert said. "That image can be explained in a number of ways. It could be a large plastic bag—"

"Shaped exactly like GOR-DON."

"Or some sort of reflection from the moon—"

"Shaped exactly like GOR-DON?"

"Or a large animal—"

"Shaped exactly like GOR-DON!"

They looked up. The entire cafeteria was silent. All eyes were on them. Alex noticed Sammi sitting alone in the far corner of the cafeteria.

"Besides," Herbert whispered, trying to ignore them. "The N.E.D. suits were destroyed."

"I never saw them destroyed," Alex said, returning his attention to Herbert.

Herbert considered this. Alex was right. They'd sent the suits back through the wormhole and trusted their closest friend in the future, a boy named Chicago, to do what they themselves didn't have the strength to do. But even if Chicago had failed . . . "There's no wormhole!" he cried. "Your father bashed it to bits!"

"Unless," Alex leaned forward and whispered, *"There's another wormhole."*

"In the Merwinsville Community Gardens? Please. Do you know what the statistical odds are for *another* wormhole popping up in our local park?"

"I'd say about the same as one popping up in a backyard tube slide."

CHAPTER 7

Alex was standing by the line of buses after school, waiting for Ellie to emerge with her fellow kindergartners, when he saw Sammi making her way toward the carpool area. He ran over to her and caught her as she approached her mom's boxy Ford minivan.

"Sammi! Hold up!" He got between her and the car, but she sidestepped him and kept going. He followed her as she continued making her way, talking as fast as he could. "Sammi, I know you're still angry and don't want to be friends, but we should talk. I really think this sighting everyone is talking about is GOR-DON, and I don't know how but he's come through a wormhole and he's here, and we should go check it out because it could be a great adventure, and there's no one I'd rather go on it with except maybe my 111-year-old self but he's not here so *whaddaya say?*"

She stopped but avoided looking at him even as he stuffed a piece of paper in her hand. "I can't," she said. "I've got jiujitsu practice now and gymnastics first thing in the morning before school."

Alex looked over her shoulder at the idling, boxy minivan waiting for her. *Honk honk!* "Oh. I didn't know you were doing all that stuff again. Maybe later, then?"

She finally looked him in the eye. "It can't be GOR-DON. I'm gonna be busy a lot from now on. I'll see ya." She turned and ran to her mom's Ford minivan. Alex watched her drive off.

Sitting in the back of the minivan, Sammi looked down and unfolded the piece of paper Alex had given her. It was the M.E.G.A. flyer. She stared closely at a very familiar-looking shape. "Mom," she said, "Is it okay if I walk through the park to my class today?"

Alex and Ellie ran as fast as they could from the bus stop on their corner to their front door. Once inside, Ellie shot like a dart straight up to her room, and Alex ran into the kitchen, looking for his parents.

"Mom! Dad! We're home! Ellie's playing in her dollhouse, and I'm gonna take my bike down to the park—"

He stopped short as he noticed a pair of handwritten notes on the counter.

Alex— I'm down at the community gardens with the rest of the M.U.L.C.H. members, making sure none of those moronic M.O.G.I.s trample our organic efforts. See that Ellie gets a snack—and anything else she wants. xoxo, MOM."

HIYA, SPORT—WENT TO MEET THE GUYS AT THE PARK TO EXPLAIN THE SIGNIFICANCE OF THIS EXTRATERRESTRIAL CONTACT TO A BUNCH OF WEEDWHACKING WHACKOS. DON'T UPSET YOUR SISTER. SEE YOU TONIGHT. –DAD.
  (P.S. IT'S M.E.G.A., NOT M.O.G.I., AND YOUR MOTHER KNOWS THAT.)

"I can't believe this!" Alex crumpled and threw the notes at the refrigerator. They bounced off a M.E.G.A. magnet (*"Keep Smiling Skyward!"*) that held the blurry flyer. He pulled it off the refrigerator and looked at it. Tossing it on the counter, he angrily poured two glasses of milk and ripped open a box of cookies. Ellie came bounding down the stairs with the latest batch of stuffed animals.

"Here," he said, shoving the box of cookies at her. "Eat a snack."

Ellie dropped her fluffy cargo and grabbed a handful of cookies, then noticed the flyer on the counter. Her eyes widened and she grabbed it, bolting out the back door. Alex heard her run into the town house and up to the second level.

"Look, Mithter Blobby Panth!" he heard her yell. *"You're famouth!"*

Alex dropped his cookie into his milk glass, then walked toward the backyard.

Sammi rolled out from under a bush, dashed to a nearby tree, and scampered up into its branches. She was dressed in her black jiujitsu *gi*, and was nearly invisible to the swarming group of Merwinsvillians who were heading toward the garden. From her perch, she made out a group of mostly men clustered outside the garden gate. They were holding all sorts of equipment—mostly expensive-looking cameras and recording devices but other things that looked like something Herbert might build in his bedroom lab. Long wands with sensors at the ends of them, metal boxes with dials and digital readout indicators, metal detectors mounted on poles. Some of them wore large headphones or goggles, and almost all of them, including Alex's dad, had on T-shirts that read: *M.E.G.A. OFFICIAL SITE INSPECTION TEAM.*

The M.E.G.A. men were pressed against the garden gate, trying to get in. On the other side, holding them back, were a group of mostly ladies dressed in gardening clothes. Many, including Alex's mom, stood arm-in-arm or held up shovels, spades, and hoes, and a banner: THIS M.U.L.C.H. SHALL NOT BE MOVED!

The two sides were yelling at each other over the fence, and from what Sammi could figure out, the M.E.G.A. men were eager to get into the garden and analyze the soil, photograph the plants, and search for anything out of the ordinary. The M.U.L.C.H. ladies were dead set against this, for the simple reason that they didn't want their vegetables trod upon. Sammi felt they both had a point.

She climbed higher in the tree to get a good look at the whole garden and spotted someone sneak around the far side of the fence line and drop over the wall, unnoticed, inside the garden.

Sammi slid down the tree and circled around the opposite side of the garden fence. She quickly scaled it, then dropped behind some large tomato plants. She belly-crawled toward a shuffling sound, then, staying low, ran toward the center.

BONK! She and Herbert slammed into each other, knocking each other down.

"What are you doing here?" Herbert asked.

Sammi didn't respond. She was looking at the ground. Herbert looked down, too, and his eyes widened. They both stood up slowly and took a step back.

In the dirt between them were the unmistakable tracks of either six very chubby garden snakes—or else the six tentacles of one very normal-sized G'Dalien.

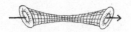

Alex entered the *Fluffy Stuff 'n' Pals Teaparty Townhouse*, his heart pounding like crazy as he tightly gripped a Wiffle ball bat. He crept up the narrow plastic staircase leading to the upper level and listened intently as Ellie chatted with what he hoped wasn't just another of her imaginary friends.

"You'll never believe what Victoria did today, Mithter Blobby Panth," he heard her say. "Victoria actually told Tommy Brookth that my behavior at *my party* wath *inappropriate*! I will never invite *her* to my tea party town houth!"

Alex reached the top of the steps and peered around the corner. From his hiding spot, he could see only half the small room, and watched as Ellie poured make-pretend tea for a very large squishy-looking stuffed octopus. Alex pulled back and exhaled, half disappointed and half amused. How many more times was this stupid dollhouse going to freak him out?

Alex lowered his weapon and stepped into the tiny room. He could now take in the entire tea party, and he froze when he saw the guest of honor, crammed in the corner. Holding a tiny teacup in front of him and wearing a giant G'Dalien-sized N.E.D. suit was the mean and nasty GOR-DON.

CHAPTER 8

Herbert and Sammi ran to the Filby house and rang the bell frantically. When no one answered, they barged in.

"Alex! Where are you?" They made their way through the house, looking everywhere, and began heading for the back deck.

"*DON'T COME OUT HERE! IT'S A TRAP!*" Alex's voice called out from the backyard. Herbert and Sammi ran out onto the porch and were immediately scooped off the ground.

"*Aaaah!*" Herbert screamed, sounding not

unlike one of Ellie's birthday party guests.

GOR-DON lifted Herbert and Sammi alongside Alex so the three were each about four feet off the ground, wrapped up like burritos within his tentacles.

"So," Alex said to the other two, "which part wasn't clear? 'Don't come out here' or 'It's a trap'?"

"Shut up," said Herbert, squirming to try and free himself.

"*MWAAA-HAA-HA-HA!*" GOR-DON laughed a horrible laugh as he slithered down the steps with his captive prey, onto the grass and over to the tea party town house. "The mighty AlienSlayers! Completely helpless in their own backyard!"

"I—I can't believe it!" Sammi said.

"Oh, believe it!" The fat G'Dalien grinned, baring his tiny, pointed teeth. He looked around. "Nice planet you have here. *Think I'll rule it.*"

WALLOP! Something large slammed GOR-DON in the side of his head. He dropped his prey and looked up to see Ellie hanging out of the upstairs tea party town house window, holding her giant stuffed octopus by its fuzzy legs. "Mithter Blobby Panth!" Ellie yelled at him. "You are a *getht* at thith tea party and mutht behave *appropriately*."

"*OOOMPH!*" GOR-DON let out a burst of air as Alex and Sammi charged him, knocking him in the belly and pinning him to the ground. He threw Sammi off him with one of his six tentacles, but Herbert had grabbed Mrs. Filby's garden hose and climbed up onto the deck. He leaped onto GOR-DON and slid down his back, roping the creature's legs with the hose. Hog-tied, the top-heavy G'Dalien crashed to the ground. Alex sat on him and pinned his tiny arms as Sammi came running up with a giant ball of Mrs. Filby's strongest garden twine. Within minutes, the three ex-AlienSlayers had GOR-DON tightly bound and squirming on Alex's lawn. They looked at one another and grinned.

"Hey, we still got it." Alex beamed.

"Yeah," Sammi said, smiling at them both. "I guess maybe we do."

"*My turn! Do me next!*" Ellie squealed from the window of her town house.

After stuffing the bound blob up the narrow staircase of Ellie's *Fluffy Stuff 'n' Pals Teaparty Townhouse*, Alex, Herbert, and Sammi managed to plop him into a tiny chair. Alex picked up his Wiffle bat and pointed it in the fat G'Dalien's face.

"All right, *Mr. Blobby Pants*," Alex said. "Start talking."

GOR-DON's eyes narrowed. He blinked. Then his waddly chin began to quiver. Suddenly the giant evil G'Dalien burst into uncontrollable sobs.

"Ohhh . . . why am I such a failure at everything I try to do? She's going to have my tentacles wrapped in rice for this! It was such a simple task, and I BLEW IT!"

He turned his head and leaned his face into the soft, fluffy belly of an overstuffed hedgehog. *PHHHHLLLLPPPPT!* He blew what would be his nose, if G'Daliens had noses. Ellie stared daggers at her rude new guest.

"You said, 'she,'" Sammi said coldly. "Who is 'she'?"

He stopped blubbering for a second and looked at them. He actually looked frightened, as if he'd said something he shouldn't have. Then he burst into tears again. *"Oh, what difference does it make?"* He wailed.

"Jeez, calm down," Alex said. "Pull yourself together, man."

GOR-DON took a deep breath. "You don't know her," he said with a sniffle. "She has weapons. Powers. And she's *mean.*"

"Who?" Herbert snapped. "Who are you talking about?"

"*AeroStar,*" GOR-DON said in a croaky near-whisper. "My queen. Supreme Leader of the universe. Or at least Future Merwinsville. She's back. With a vengeance. Specifically, a vengeance against you three."

"Us?" Alex said. "Why us? We don't even know this Avatar."

"*AeroStar*," GOR-DON corrected him. "And she knows you. In the beginning she promised if I helped her bring chaos and fear between the humans and G'Daliens, she'd let me run things. I'd be ruler of Merwinsville, which would impress Marion, who'd *come crawling back to me and*—" He stopped and looked around nervously. "I command you to forget I said that last part."

"Okay," said Alex. "'Cause that got weird. Even for you."

"So this *AeroStar* was behind all those evil plans of yours we thwarted?"

The blobby beast nodded. "I hated you for it. But it *really* ticked *her* off."

"But we were only trying to defeat *your* stupid, evil plans," Sammi said.

"Well, unfortunately for you, my stupid, evil plans were part of *her* master evil plan."

"Which was?"

"To get revenge against the G'Daliens. They ruined her life, so naturally she had to exact vengeance upon them."

"She's pretty big on the whole vengeance thing, huh?" Alex asked.

"You have no idea," GOR-DON continued. "She recruited me to get the humans to fear them. But you three ruined that plan. And then she instructed me to get the Klapthorians to invade, thinking the G'Daliens would flee as they did their own planet. But you got in the way of that one, too. That was the last straw. My queen shifted her revenge to the AlienSlayers—an all-new, Three-and-a-Half-Point Plan of Vengeance designed to get back at you, once and for all."

"What could she possibly do to us?" Herbert asked.

"Yeah, what's her plan?" Sammi added.

"I get information only on a need-to-know basis. But it doesn't matter. My arrival here marks the beginning of her plan, so it's already too late. Too late to save Future Merwinsville, too late to save the G'Daliens, too late to save all their technological inventions—*too late for you, SlayerFakers, to do anything to stop her. MWAH-HAHAHAHAHAHA!*"

"Actually," Alex said, "we could take the N.E.D. suits off you, travel to the future, kick this AeroStar lady's butt, save Future Merwinsville, and become heroes again. It's kinda what we do."

"You'd be in so much trouble with her," Sammi added.

GOR-DON stopped laughing and looked at them. Alex, Herbert, and Sammi were eyeing his silver outfit, looking at the crude stitches he'd made to turn the three human-sized suits into one G'Dalien-sized suit. "It would never work," he said nervously. "Y-you don't know where the wormhole is! You said yourself it was destroyed. The new one could be anywhere on this sorry excuse you call a—"

Click. WUBBA-WUBBA-WUBBA-WUBBA . . .

Sammi had casually reached out and flipped the switch on GOR-DON's sewn-together N.E.D. suit. On the wall directly behind GOR-DON's fat, stubbly head, a large, ornate-looking but fake decal mirror over a fake decal mantel and fireplace began to shimmer and ripple a bright blue. It pulled GOR-DON, tied to his chair, toward it, slamming his head on the low ceiling.

Sammi switched off the pulsating wormhole. "Whaddya know? There it is," she said.

"Son of a Kroflex," GOR-DON said.

"Of course." Herbert walked over and touched the fake mirror. "This isn't a 'new' wormhole. It never left this place. It was never in the tube slide. It exists in space. Right here." He tapped the fake mirror sticker on the plastic wall. "The jungle gym, and now this dollhouse, were just built around it. It's always been here. I really should've known that."

Alex stepped up to GOR-DON, holding a large pair of scissors menacingly. "We're gonna need that suit, *Mister Blobby-Pants*."

The three retired AlienSlayers huddled outside the tea party town house, looking down at the giant sewn-together N.E.D. suit lying in a heap at their feet.

"We don't even know if this AeroStar person actually exists," Sammi said. "GOR-DON could be bluffing. It is GOR-DON, after all."

"But what if he's not," Alex said. "You heard him. He said the entire city's in danger. The humans, the G'Daliens—"

"Their technology . . . ," Herbert added.

"I'm worried, too," she said. "But what if it's a trap?"

"We're AlienSlayers," Alex said. "There isn't a trap that could trap us."

Herbert rolled his eyes, then picked up his helmet where he'd dropped it earlier and looked at it sadly. "If only I were smart enough to get this to work, we could see what's going on, through Old Man Herbert's eyes."

Alex glanced over to a very confused Sammi. "It's his P.U.P.E.," Alex said. Ignoring the fact that this explanation made Sammi even more confused as well as a little grossed out, Alex continued. "C'mon, guys. Let's not overthink things here."

"Yes. Why start now?" Herbert said.

"N.E.D. suits. *Check*. Wormhole. *Check*. Helpless victims who need saving. *Checkarooni*. Ridiculously awesome adventure, ripe for the plucking. *Check-a-doodle-doo*. It's a win, win, win . . . win . . . See? I lost track of all the wins!"

"I don't know," Sammi said. "I've just got a very bad, very strange feeling about this. There's something's fishy about it."

"The only thing fishy is Sadsack Squidpants up

there. And we've got him tied up and telling us all we need to know to successfully pull off this mission."

"Which brings up a logistical question," Herbert said. "We can't leave GOR-DON under the watchful eyes of a five-year-old and her dollhouse full of stuffed animals. If we go, one of us will need to stay behind and G'Dalien-sit."

Alex shook his head. "Don't look at me! I'm out of the babysitting biz. No way I'm missing this."

Herbert and Sammi looked at each other. "You go with him," Sammi said. "I haven't exactly been a part of the team lately, anyway. Go find out what's really going on and report back. Then we'll figure out what, if anything, we should do. I'll stay here and hold down the"—she looked up at Ellie's *Fluffy Stuff 'n' Pals Teaparty Townhouse*—"whatever this thing is supposed to be."

"*Yes!*" Alex exclaimed. "AlienSlayers reunited!" He held up his hands to both Herbert and Sammi, waiting for their high-fives. Herbert sneered, then saw Sammi smile. He reached up and barely touched Alex's hand.

"*There it is!*" Alex exclaimed. "*That's* what I'm talkin' about!"

Alex picked up the silvery sewn-together pile of N.E.D. suits and threw them around his and Herbert's shoulders. "This is gonna be so awesome," he said.

Herbert stared straight at Sammi, who couldn't help but giggle at them both.

Upstairs in the town house, GOR-DON sat tied up with a sad, distant look on his face. *"Oh, Marion."* He sighed. *"My mission didn't go exactly as planned, but hopefully I can still win you back—OWEEE!"*

Sammi had entered and yanked the twine, binding him to the chair extra tight. "Sorry," she said. "Can't have you going skulking off." She tied double knots and made sure he was securely fastened. "Gonna be just the two of us hanging together up here for a bit, if you wanna talk about it."

"Talk about what?"

"You and Marion. I almost lost a couple good friends, too. I know it can hurt."

"Please. Talk? To a human? Why would I waste my breath talking to a species that isn't worth the slime I secrete from my tentacles?"

"Well, for starters, you obviously don't feel that way about *all* of my species."

GOR-DON's angry expression drooped. He blinked at Sammi and watched as she headed down the narrow town house stairs.

On the first floor, Herbert was trying to figure a way to take apart the huge refitted N.E.D. suit and separate it back into three human-sized suits.

"Just leave it as is," Alex said. "You might rip it. Besides, we can both fit in it together. It'll be more fun that way, too."

"I try to avoid physical contact with other humans," Herbert said.

"Oh. Well, just think of me as some kind of algae you'd grow in one of your test tubes."

"Done."

A few minutes later, once Alex had instructed Ellie to obey Sammi and help her keep an eye on Mr. Blobby Pants, he and his traveling buddy stood before the fake decal mirror wrapped in the giant silver, sewn-together N.E.D. suit. Sammi stepped up and gave each of them a kiss on the cheek.

"For luck," she said. "And friendship."

"And adventure!" Alex said.

Even Herbert couldn't hide his excitement. "And science," he added.

Alex grinned as he hit the switches on the conjoined N.E.D. suits. They turned to face the fake decal mirror above the fake decal fireplace. A shimmering, silver-blue surface rippled in the wall, making the fake, silvery mirror look like a liquid blue lake someone had thrown a very large stone into. The entire tea party town house began to vibrate, and the wormhole made a very loud, pulsing sound.... *WUBBA-WUBBA-WUBBA-WUBBA-WUBBA!*

FOOMPH! Alex and Herbert were suddenly sucked off their feet and straight into the liquidlike portal. A second later, the wormhole disappeared, the tea house stopped vibrating—and Alex and Herbert were gone.

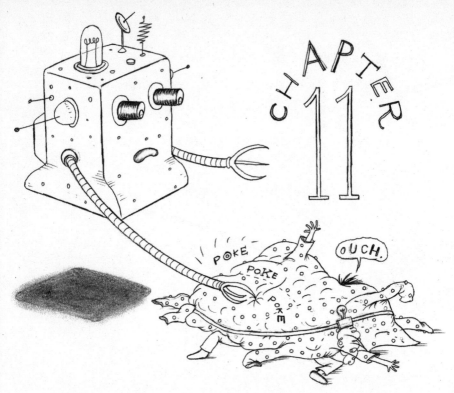

POP! Alex and Herbert had gotten so wrapped up in the giant N.E.D. suit during their quick journey through the wormhole that they came flying out in a large silver lump. Tangled and completely covered by the suit, they hit a soft, sandy floor and immediately froze as they heard a horrible laugh.

"They're here!" an old woman's voice shrieked. "Just as I planned! MinionBot—bring the Alien-Slayers to me!"

Alex heard a mechanical whirring near his head, and then felt a heavy robotic claw touch his arm through the suit. As it poked and prodded them, Herbert and Alex knew instinctively to lie quietly. *"Stay still,"* a tinny voice whispered from just outside the N.E.D. suit. *"Don't move, no matter what."*

The MinionBot hovered over the silver lump lying on the floor of a scene Alex and Herbert knew well. It was a fake caveman diorama, complete with a fake woolly mammoth, caveman mannequins, and a fake rock with a fake painted-black cave entrance. It was this fake cave entrance that housed the other end of the wormhole, where they'd just popped out.

This was one of many dioramas in the Hallway of Human History, a long series of lifelike scenes located inside the enormous Museum of Human History. The museum had been built by the G'Daliens and housed artifacts and information showing how the G'Daliens came to help the human race. It was a monument to the friendship between two species who had chosen to live together in peace.

But now, even hidden under the N.E.D. suit, Alex and Herbert could sense that some horrible changes had happened since they'd left Future

Merwinsville. For one thing, the secret fake cave entrance to the wormhole was obviously no longer a secret. For another, the place was swarming with MinionBots.

The Bot that had whispered to Alex and Herbert quickly scanned the oversized N.E.D. suit, prodded its contents, then finally turned to face its master. "I have good news, your Awesomeness," they heard the Bot's mechanized voice report. "The three AlienSlayers have perished during their journey here. By my analysis, the faulty Negative Energy Densifyer suit failed to protect their humanoid bodies. All that remains are small lumps of fleshy goo. Congratulations. Ultimate vengeance is yours, my queen!"

"*WHAT?*" The old woman's voice screeched so loudly it made Alex and Herbert shiver beneath their N.E.D. blanket. "I never intended for them to *die*! This was not part of my plan! My plan was to exact a horrible vengeance on them! Death would be too kind! *Bring them to me!*"

"That is not advised, your Mega-ness," the MinionBot said. "The charred, lumpy remnants of the subjects give off a most disgusting stench."

"*He means you,*" Alex whispered. Herbert poked him to shut up.

"Since when do my mechanized minions talk back or offer their opinions?" The old woman's voice sternly ordered, "*BRING ME THE STENCHY LUMPS.*"

The MinionBot slowly scooped up the silver-bundled Alex and Herbert in its arms and glided over to the feet of the fake woolly mammoth. Its robotic arms extended, lifting them toward a wrinkled old hand that reached down from atop the mammoth. Its bony finger poked at the blobs that were Alex and Herbert.

Inside the N.E.D. suit, Herbert was jabbed in the cheek by the probing digit. Alex put his hand over Herbert's mouth before he could say, "*Ouch!*" Doing this allowed access to the most ticklish section of Alex's entire body—his armpit.

The finger poked his armpit and he jumped. He began giggling uncontrollably. "*Heeeeehaaahaaa— stop it! Haaaheeeee!*"

One more tickling jab to Alex's underarm and he doubled over in a fit of giggles, jerking his body wildly. They both rolled out of the N.E.D. suit, off the end of the MinionBot's arms, and onto the floor at the feet of the stuffed woolly mammoth.

As the MinionBots circled them, Alex and Herbert cast their stare past them, up the mammoth's leg, to find glaring back down the face of a very mean-looking old woman. An ornate, golden tiara sat atop her long black-and-gray-streaked hair. Alex noticed she had freckles on her

wrinkled old cheeks, and he thought there was something familiar about this old lady. She stared at them another second—then she slowly smiled. That's when he recognized her.

She leaped off her mammoth-throne, did a double-flip in the air, and landed heavily right next to their heads. It was a surprisingly acrobatic woolly mammoth dismount, considering the woman had to be at least 111 years old. She straightened the golden tiara on her head, which matched the golden star on her black bodysuit. She also sported a long flowing, golden cape, which Alex couldn't help but be impressed by.

"That's a nice cape . . . *Sammi.*"

"*SILENCE!*" she shrieked back at him. "No one's *dared* call me that in years. I go by a different name. I'm known—and feared—as *AEROSTAR!*"

She looked up at her small audience of MinionBots staring stupidly near the mouth of the fake cave. "I said, '*AEROSTAR*'!"

The MinionBots reacted jerkily with a dull, "Yaaaaaaay," followed by a round of tinny applause as they banged their metal claws together unenthusiastically.

"Idiots," she muttered with a look of disgust. "But speaking of Sammi, where is she? *All three of you* were supposed to come here. That was the plan. Didn't that moron G'Dalien tell you the city was in danger, the G'Daliens exiled, blah blah blah?"

"So it's true?" Alex said.

"*So it's true?*" AeroStar repeated mockingly to Alex. "You want to know if I actually sent your dear old version of yourself away forever, along with the entire G'Dalien race? And you"—she turned to Herbert—"*you* undoubtedly want to know if it's true that I've destroyed all the G'Dalien technological wonders you so adore."

"What have you done?" Herbert said, his eyes narrowing.

"You'll have plenty of time to find out," she said. "In fact, once my Three-and-a-Half-Point Plan of Vengeance is complete, the two of you will have the rest of your miserable lives to suffer all that I've done. *HAHAHAHAHAHAHAHA!*"

She cackled for a moment, until she realized that

she was the only one laughing. She stopped and looked around at the MinionBots. *"You're supposed to join in with my evil laugh, you metallic morons!"*

The MinionBots burst into flat, robotic laughter: "Ha. Ha. Ha. Ha. Ha. Ha—"

"ENOUGH!" she barked. (They stopped immediately.) "I hate these robots. I honestly don't know why I had my company create them. Oh, wait, yes I do," she said casually. *"MinionBots, seize them."*

AeroStar snatched the oversized N.E.D. suit, reached up to her Utility Tiara and pressed a button. Tiny jets clicked out the sides of it and emitted a small turboblast, propelling her into the air. She backflipped onto her woolly mammoth throne and sat back to watch as the MinionBots closed in on

Alex and Herbert, their retractable claws reaching out menacingly.

Herbert ignored the impending danger and instead stared up at AeroStar's tiara, impressed. "See, now *that's* a good invention," he muttered.

"HEADS UP, SLEWG!" Alex grabbed Herbert's head and shoved it down just as a MinionBot lurched for them. They ducked under its claw and then sidestepped as the Bot crashed into another that was moving in fast. As a few of them got their

retractable arms tangled up, Alex and Herbert hit the sandy floor and rolled beneath their floating metal bodies, making a beeline for the Hallway of Human History.

"YOU IDIOTS!" AeroStar shrieked. "Get them! *GET THEM!"*

She was about to fire up her Utility Tiara and go after them herself when a MinionBot said, "Please. Leave it to me, your Fearsomeness." The robot blasted off, whooshing after them, down the Hallway of Human History.

Alex was panting as he tried to keep up with Herbert. "Wait! Where are we going? We have to steal those suits and get back to Sammi!"

"I know, and we will!" Herbert called back as they skidded around a corner and headed for the main lobby of the museum. "I just have to see for myself first—*I have to know what she's done!*"

Alex kept running, even as a sick feeling rose in his stomach. The museum looked different—rundown, dirty—as if no one had worked in or visited it in a long while. "Herbert, I've got a really bad feeling ab—*OOOF!*"

"*GOTCHA!*" The MinionBot zoomed in from behind and scooped them up just as they reached the massive main lobby. Alex and Herbert kicked and squirmed but couldn't free themselves from the bot's thick mechanical arms.

To their surprise, instead of turning around and taking them back to AeroStar, the bot sped up, flying headlong straight at the giant entrance doors to the museum. "Duck your heads!" its mechanical voice yelled to them. *KA-CHUNG!* It blasted the doors open and zoomed out of the museum, soaring skyward. Alex and Herbert looked back at the museum, which was as shabby on the outside as it was on the inside. The carved words on the entrance were covered with a banner that read, *CLEMCORP HEADQUARTERS—TRESPASSERS WILL BE PROSECUTED.*

Before Alex or Herbert could figure out what was going on, the flying bot began to make strange noises. With a series of whirs and clicks, its other parts shifted and rearranged, locking into place to form a familiar design: Old Man Herbert's flying airchair. And sitting in the chair, flying it from the armrest control panel, was Old Man Herbert, Herbert's 111-year-old parallel-event-path self.

"Whoa! That was awesome, dude!" Alex exclaimed.

"Thanks," Old Man Herbert said. "Yes, I was able to make some adjustments to my airchair before AeroStar began her destruction. Whaddya think, Herbie?"

Herbert didn't answer. He was looking out at Future Merwinsville. Alex looked, too, and couldn't believe what he saw. The once-beautiful and pristine city was now a torn-down, ugly place. All the incredible structures designed and built by the G'Daliens were either gone or demolished. Huge machines smashed their way through the city, further destroying anything that was the product of the friendly aliens who had once lived alongside humans. The machines had enormous long planks of metal jutting off them like rusty steel diving boards. Hovering beneath the planks were giant magnetized metal spheres. Alex and Herbert watched in horror as a sphere zoomed down the underside of the plank and crashed into what was left of Merwinsville City Hall—the old home of their SlayerLair. On the side of the magnetic wreckers was a logo: CLEMCORP MAGNAWRECKERS.

"It's horrible," Alex said.

"Worse than I thought," Herbert added.

"I'm sorry, boys," Old Man Herbert said, veering toward a demolished stadium. "But I'm afraid it gets a lot worse."

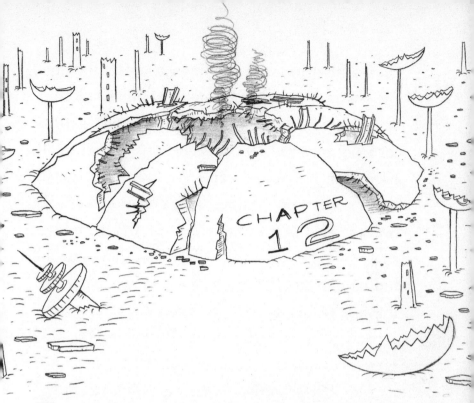

The crumbled pile of rubble and twisted metal that was once the Flee-a-seum, a giant Roman-style event stadium, looked dead and depressing from the outside. Old Man Herbert navigated his airchair up and over the jutting metal beams and flew through a small entrance hole in a slab of wall, taking Alex and Herbert inside. They circled over what had once been the magnificent stadium field and landed on the ground.

The two retired AlienSlayers hopped off the airchair and stared in awe at their surroundings:

thousands of humans camping out and hiding from the destruction going on outside. The conditions weren't great, but Alex noticed they weren't at a loss for food: hundreds of pizza boxes were stacked all over the place. Some people had even constructed small shelters out of them. Kids and grown-ups all over the field were eating pizza. If it weren't for the shabby conditions and the fact that they were all hiding like rats in a giant broken-down coliseum, it would've looked like the biggest pizza party ever. Especially because they were all enjoying the best pizza in this or any century: Andretti's.

Alex looked around. "Where are the G'Daliens?"

"AeroStar," Old Man Herbert said.

"What did she do with them?" Herbert said.

"You recall how the G'Daliens had fled their home planet and came to Earth decades ago because of those alien-bullies, the Klapthorians?"

"Yeah, and I also recall how we helped the G'Daliens kick those Klapthorians' buggy butts when they tried to do it again on this planet," Alex said.

"Precisely. What you three did was give the G'Daliens back their confidence. Many of our alien friends dreamed of going back to their home planet once they had nothing to fear and the humans were happy and comfortable with all the technological wonders they'd been given."

Herbert looked around at the destroyed Flee-a-seum, a marvel of a structure he'd seen the G'Daliens create with his own eyes. "Let me guess. She offered them a way to go home."

"She tricked us all. Won everyone over, human and G'Dalien alike. And she had a ship. A giant vessel, bigger than a Klapthorian Death Cruiser. She promised the G'Daliens safe passage back to their home planet. She promised the humans that she could build a wormhole connecting the two planets. And she promised us all that we would stay friends forever and visit each other whenever we wanted to. There was a massive parade—you know how G'Daliens like their parades. They all boarded the S.S. *Clemtanic* and she shipped them off."

Alex and Herbert stared at the old scientist, wondering the same thing. Old Man Herbert shook his head. "I tracked the ship as long as I could. My belief is she gave the ship just enough fuel to shoot them out of the earth's gravitational orbit before it died—leaving them powerless, to drift in space forever."

The sick feeling Alex had in his stomach back at the museum had now quadrupled. There was something he needed to know, but he was afraid to hear the answer. He took a deep breath. "Did any . . . humans go with them?"

Alex knew by the look on Old Man Herbert's face that his worst fear was true. "I'm so sorry, Alex. You rescued your 111-year-old parallel-universe self from that cave on the moon and showed him an adventure that was better than any video game. You opened his eyes to all the adventures of the universe. And after you left, he was eager to start a new one." Old Man Herbert paused. "AeroStar offered Old Man Alex the opportunity to captain the *S.S. Clemtanic.* He jumped at the chance."

Alex shut his eyes and tried to swallow the lump he felt growing in his throat.

"But why?" Herbert asked. "Why would she do all of this?"

"Revenge," Old Man Herbert said. "Against the three of you. I don't know what she has up her sleeve, but shipping the G'Daliens off, destroying everything they invented and gave to us, even getting rid of Old Man Alex, it's all part of her plan."

"I don't get it," Alex said. "Sammi—the Sammi *we* know—would never do these horrible things. How could they be so different? What happened to her?"

"This isn't the Sammi you know. She may have started out the same way, but different decisions, circumstances, and choices can take the same people on an infinite number of parallel-event paths—and create wildly different outcomes.

"This Sammi didn't learn the value of fun, because she never met the two of you. She worked very hard and became very successful. As a young woman, she created CLEMCORP—a company that built machines that built entire cities. Amazing technology, actually. But horrible for the

93

environment. Soon the cities created or enhanced by CLEMCORP became so polluted they were nearly uninhabitable. That's when the G'Daliens came and cleaned everything up. It destroyed her corporation, and drove her crazy that there was a superior technology to hers."

"So she tried to get vengeance against the G'Daliens?" Herbert asked.

"She used GOR-DON, a mean, hateful, slow-witted G'Dalien, to carry out her plans while she continued to build bigger and more destructive machines on another planet. He did his best but always failed. At first because of his own stupidity, and later because of, well, three kids who came from another time."

"We thought we were just keeping GOR-DON from being a jerk," Alex said. "We didn't know we were messing with an all-powerful mega-evil-future-Sammi lady."

"Well, unfortunately she didn't take your ignorance into account. After you left, she came back, won over all of us, then worked quickly to seek her vengeance against you. Given the most recent events, I'd theorize that isn't over yet."

They sat there in silence for a moment, letting all this soak in. Finally, Alex stood up. "Okay. We need to get those suits and go back to Present Day Merwinsville before AeroStar does," he said. "Sammi doesn't know any of this. She could be in danger. Then the three of us need to come here and do what we do: make it right."

Herbert thought about this. "Wait," he said. "Something else doesn't compute. AeroStar isn't going to travel to the present to get Sammi. She wants Sammi to come *here*. Think about it. She had the suits. She could've come to us anytime she wanted. But she didn't—she sent the Blubbering Blob instead, to trick the three of us into coming to *her*."

Alex blinked, then said something he really didn't enjoy saying to Herbert. "You're right. If only we had some way of communicating with her, to tell her what's going on. Something like your P.U.P.E.-helmety thing."

Herbert looked at Old Man Herbert. "He's talking about my failed attempt to finish what you and I started: the Parallel Universe Perspective Enhancer. I'm . . . sorry I couldn't make mine work."

"It wouldn't have mattered," Old Man Herbert said. "I was still working on mine—an eyeshade-visor prototype—the day Old Man Alex found out he'd be captaining the S.S. *Clemtanic*. He came to my lab to tell me the good news. He said it was a perfect opportunity for him because not only could he overcome his old fear of G'Daliens that drove him into hiding in the first place, but he'd have the chance to see the galaxy. He said he was most excited to fly right past the sun. I suppose it was because he'd lived for so long on the dark side of the moon. After he left, I couldn't find the eyeshade-visor prototype. I'm pretty sure he swiped it to use as sunglasses." He paused. "I was angry at first, of course, but I'm happy he got to take them, as a good-bye gift. I'd installed a working SuperCheezyFrankOnnaStickerator 3000 machine on the ship because I knew he'd get hungry on the journey. But I'm glad he stole my invention, even if he thought they were just a pair of cool shades."

Old Man Herbert put his hand on Alex's shoulder. "For what it's worth, we'd become very good friends, he and I. And that's all thanks to you."

Alex nodded, but a rush of thoughts were running through his head as he looked out at the sun setting beyond the twisted metal jutting out of the top of the ruined Flee-a-seum.

Sammi stood in Alex's backyard, staring at the sky. The sun was setting, and she was growing concerned about Herbert and Alex. How long does it take to travel a hundred years into the future, see if a giant G'Dalien was lying about an evil queen who'd supposedly destroyed the entire city, and then come back?

"They'd better not have stopped for one of Alex's Mega-Choco-Bomb Marshmallow Root Beer Smoothies," she said to herself. She allowed herself to smile at this, but only for a moment. She knew she couldn't keep GOR-DON hidden in a tea party town house forever. What if Alex's parents came home? How would she explain where Alex and Herbert were? She began to half wish she was at her jiujitsu class perfecting her triangle choke submission setup with her instructor, Sensei Ed.

Of course this wasn't really true. If Future Merwinsvillians were in trouble, she'd want to help them, right? "Right," she said to herself as she walked back to the giant dollhouse. She found GOR-DON sitting in his little chair, staring blankly out at the same sunset. But something was different. She glanced down and saw his bindings had slipped off and were lying on the floor at his feet.

Thinking fast, Sammi quickly grabbed Alex's Wiffle ball bat and lurched toward GOR-DON. "Don't make any sudden moves!" she said. "I mean it! *I will Wiffle the ugly outta you!*"

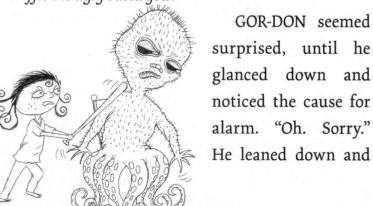

GOR-DON seemed surprised, until he glanced down and noticed the cause for alarm. "Oh. Sorry." He leaned down and slipped his ropes back up over his belly. Then he sighed heavily and stared out the window again.

Sammi lowered the yellow plastic weapon and took another step toward him. His belly heaved as he drew a long, deep breath. "Ever wonder what you were meant to do with your life?" he finally said.

Sammi eyed him carefully. "Er, sure. I guess."

"I mean, what am I doing?" GOR-DON looked down at the loose-fitting twine hanging off his tentacles. "I'm ordered to make this suit, go through the wormhole, tell you guys what's going on in the future, and get you to rush back into a trap. And what do I do? I get myself captured *and* lose the suits." He sighed again.

"Wait—*it's a trap?*" Sammi's eyes were wide with worry.

"Of course it's a trap. But I couldn't even get that right. *All three of you* were supposed to go through. She was very specific about that. And I blew it. Which means"—his big bulging eyes began watering up again—"*I can't see Marion ever again. . . . AeroStar will destroy me if I go back!*"

"Forget what she'll do to you! What's she going to do to my friends, you big creep?"

"*Oh, Marion!*" he blubbered into his tentacle. "It was all for you! I only planted the alien podseeds so I could save this wretched town then bring you here to show you I was a hero—but now it's all ruined!" *SPLORK!* He turned his head and blew his nose-holes into a nearby stuffed armadillo.

"*Hey!*" Ellie grabbed the armadillo away from him and took it down the stairs to clean the alien-snot off it.

Sammi glared at GOR-DON. "Now you listen to me, you oversize space slug. You'd better— Hold up. What was that part about planting *alien podseeds?*"

Before GOR-DON could answer, Sammi heard two cars pull into the driveway. Then she heard two car doors slam shut. Then she heard two grown-up voices from inside Alex's house. Then the hair stood up on her neck.

"*Alex! Ellie? Where are you two?*" It was Mrs. Filby, followed by her husband.

"*Champ? Ell-Bell? You guys okay?*"

Sammi looked through the town house window as Mr. and Mrs. Filby stepped out onto the back deck. Thinking quickly, she shoved GOR-DON, knocking him backward in his tiny chair. He looked up at her.

"What'd you do that for?"

"Shh!" She put her finger over her lips and peeked through the window. The Filbys were crossing the lawn, heading for the entrance to the town house.

"Oh, good," Mr. Filby said. "They figured out how to unlock the door. I thought I was going to have to take my blowtorch to this thing."

Just as he put his hand on the big goofy doorknob, the door slammed open. Sammi burst out with a big frozen smile on her face.

"Hi, Mr. and Mrs. Filby! Uh, Alex just ran over to Herbert's to pick some more flowers. We thought it'd be nice to spruce up Ellie's new place. Kind of our birthday gift to her. They'll both be back, er, at some point, in the near future."

"You kids are so sweet," Mrs. Filby said. "You take your time." She looked down and noticed Ellie standing beside Sammi. "Sweetie, listen to Mommy. There's a little bit of a situation down at the community gardens, and Mommy's M.U.L.C.H. group is organizing an overnight sit-in. I'll be camping out down there, so I need you to be a good girl for Daddy—"

"Uh, hold up there," Mr. Filby interjected. He turned his attention to his daughter. "Actually, Ellie-Bell, it's *Daddy* who has to go down to the park

for the night. He and his fellow M.E.G.A. Men are staging a level-six mandatory night vigil. It's all hands on deck, so you stay here with Mommy and I'll see you in the morn—"

Before he could finish, Mrs. Filby suddenly dashed into the house and began riffling through the downstairs closet. Answering her challenge, Mr. Filby bolted into the garage. They began yelling at each other through the walls as they clattered around for whatever they were looking for.

"I called it first, *Daryl!*" Mrs. Filby shouted as she threw things into the hallway, looking for her sleeping bag. "Which means you need to stay, because Alex isn't old enough to watch Ellie overnight!"

"I don't think protecting the community gardens is quite as important as welcoming an alien visitor into the *actual community—SUSAN!*" Mr. Filby hollered back over the clanging of various objects as he searched for his camping gear.

Ellie looked up at the top window of her town house. GOR-DON peeked down at her. The little girl scowled at him, then turned to Sammi standing dumbfounded on the lawn. "All right, lithen up," the five-year-old whispered menacingly. "I'll keep them away for the night. You get that dithguthting thad thack out of my town houth and back wherever he came from, or I'll blow the whole operathon wide open. You read me, thithter?" She shot GOR-DON a look. "You wore out your welcome, *Blubberbutt*. I'm the landlady around here, and *you—are—evicted*."

She spun around on her tiny heel and ran into the house, yelling after her parents. "Mommy! Daddy! I wanna camp, too! *I wanna caaaaaammp!*"

Minutes later, Sammi stood waving at the front door, watching Mr. and Mrs. Filby ride off, each of their cars filled with sleeping bags, backpacks, energy bars, and flashlights. Ellie looked back from the car seat in her mother's car. Sipping on a juice box, she shot Sammi a look that said, *Don't meth with me.*

Relieved, Sammi shut the door, walked back outside and up the stairs of the *Fluffy Stuff 'n' Pals Teaparty Townhouse.* She climbed the steps, stepped into the small room—and froze in her tracks.

GOR-DON was gone.

As darkness began to fall over Future Merwinsville, Alex, Herbert, and Old Man Herbert sat high atop the twisted beams that formed a crude roof to the demolished Flee-a-seum. Old Man Herbert had flown them up there to get a look at the destruction, but Alex had his gaze fixed on the stars beginning to appear overhead.

"I'm so sorry, Alex," Herbert said.

"It's not true," Alex said.

Herbert stared at Alex, knowing this was one time when his knowledge of statistics and probability ratios wouldn't be appreciated. Instead, he turned to Old Man Herbert. "Is there any chance he and the G'Daliens are out there somewhere?" Herbert asked.

"The S.S. *Clemtanic* powered down and disappeared from my grid soon after exiting the earth's orbit," he said. "I lost the signal shortly after that. If there was a powering-up or a restart of some kind, I would've picked it up. It's been silent for a long, long time, I'm afraid."

"*It's not true*," Alex repeated.

"I know you're upset," Herbert said. "We all are. But facts and logic dictate—"

"I heard the facts, and I don't care about the logic," Alex shot back. "Because I know my friend. He's a hero. An honorary AlienSlayer. Old Man Alex would never just float away in space and let all his new G'Dalien friends *die*." He shot them a determined look. "It's not true, and I'm going to find them."

"Alex, you have to listen to reason," Old Man Herbert tried to explain. "The galaxy is extremely vast. Pinpointing anything out there, even a ship the size of the S.S. *Clemtanic*, would be like looking for a single molecule of water in an entire ocean."

"There's one person who could show me," Alex said to Old Man Herbert. "And hopefully he's still wearing the gift you gave him."

"What are you talking about?" Herbert asked.

"If you could get your P.U.P.E. helmet to work, it could allow the wearer to see what's being looked at through Old Man Herbert's P.U.P.E. sunglasses, right?"

"Why does he keep saying that word?" Old Man Herbert asked.

"*If* it were to work," Herbert explained, "the wearers would have to be the parallel universe versions of the *same person*." He gestured toward Old Man Herbert. "For example, I could only share perspective with him."

"Yes, but *he* doesn't have his glasses. Old Man Alex does. And so the only person who could put on your helmet and see whatever he's looking at is—"

"You," Old Man Herbert said. "That's exactly right."

"It doesn't matter," Herbert said. "My helmet is sitting on your back deck, a hundred years in the past from where we are now. And I couldn't get it to work, remember?"

"Well, maybe it's time for someone else to take a stab at it, Slewgy." Alex looked at Old Man Herbert. "How 'bout a crash course in Parallel Universe Perspective Enhancement, professor?"

"*What?*" Herbert scoffed.

Old Man Herbert was slightly taken aback. "I must say, Alex, I am impressed you know your terminology."

"It's P.U.P.E.," Alex said. "What's hard to know?"

Suddenly, a bright beam of light blasted through the darkness, blinding the three of them. "*POSITIVE IDENTIFICATION CONFIRMED. FUGITIVES DETECTED.*"

The MinionBot's BioScanner blinked off, and they saw its chest plate pop open. Old Man Herbert shot straight up in his airchair just as something sprang out of the MinionBot's chest. In an instant, Alex and Herbert found themselves caught up in a strong, netlike fabric. It pulled tightly around them, yanking them off the girder they were standing on. They swung out over the city as the MinionBot turned to carry them off when— *CHUNGHK!* Something slammed into it.

Flying in his airchair, Old Man Herbert

maneuvered back around for another hit at the bot. *CHUNGHK!* He bashed into it again, knocking it back toward the Flee-a-seum, where it hobbled in midair near the crisscrossing girders, high above the field below. *CHUNGHK!* This hit caused the line holding the net to snap. Herbert and Alex screamed as they dropped like an anchor until the net caught on a steel rod jutting out. They hung there, hundreds of feet over the field, like a couple of freshly caught tuna.

"Hang on, boys! I'll get you!" Old Man Herbert yelled as he circled around and zoomed for them. *CHUNGHK!* Before he could reach them, the MinionBot flew out of nowhere and slammed into him. The two heaps of flying metal stayed connected as they skidded off a large slab of wall, out of sight over the far side of the Flee-a-seum.

CREEEAAAAK! The thin steel rod holding Alex and Herbert like a fishing pole began to bend under their weight. The two of them held their breath as it bowed downward slowly, slowly, until— *SPROING!*—it snapped back, releasing its catch.

Herbert and Alex screamed as they flew through the air. They clung to each other as they soared through the night sky. Suddenly, they jerked to a stop. Relieved that they weren't splattered on the ground, they looked up. As happy as they were not to be piles of goo, they were horrified to see a

MinionBot towing them above the ruined city of Merwinsville, hauling them toward the museum. Their stomachs dropped as they looked back, hoping to spot some sign of Old Man Herbert. But all they saw were the caved-in walls of the Flee-a-seum fading in the darkness.

Sammi ran around the cul-de-sac, peering into hedges and driveways, searching for a lost and somewhat emotionally wounded G'Dalien.

"*GOR-DON!*" she whispered. "*Come out! We can talk about it!*"

She was thankful that all the M.E.G.A. members were down at the park, but still, this was a quiet neighborhood, and a giant squidlike monster would not go over well. She imagined how this would upset the Merwinsville Neighbors Association as she peeked into Mr. Doherty's toolshed.

"Hi there, Sammi." Mr. Doherty's voice made her jump. He was suddenly standing right behind her, with an armful of trash he was taking out to his garbage bin. "Need to borrow something?"

"Uh, no, Mr. Doherty, thanks. Just, uh, looking for my cat—uh, GOR-DON."

Mr. Doherty lifted the lid to the bin and, without looking, emptied his trash bucket into it. Sammi's eyes grew wide as she saw GOR-DON staring up at her, crammed inside the garbage bin.

"Oh. I didn't realize you had a cat," Mr. Doherty said as he unwittingly covered a fat, blobby G'Dalien with his garbage. He slammed the lid back down on GOR-DON's head. "Well, I'll keep an eye out for— *Gorgon*, was it?"

"Close enough. Thanks, Mr. D."

"What's he look like? Siamese? Tabby?"

"Uh, mix-breed. Six feet tall, tentacles, about three hundred pounds."

Mr. Doherty stared at her for a moment. "I'll, uh, keep my eyes peeled."

She thanked him and watched as he went back into his house. As soon as it was clear, she opened the garbage-bin lid and looked down on GOR-DON, who was curled up in a ball among the trash. "What are you doing in there?" she said.

BEING IN HERE COMFORTS ME. LEAVE ME ALONE.

"I *can't*! If you're discovered, they'll kill you! And I need to know what you've done! You have to get out of there—"

Suddenly, a voice stopped her cold. It was a voice she *really* didn't want to hear.

"Look, you guys! Isn't that the *world-famous* AlienSlayer?"

Sammi slammed down the lid and spun around

just as Moose, Adriana, and a few of their hooligan pals came skidding to a stop on their bikes in front of Sammi.

"It's a school night, Moosie," Sammi said. "Isn't it past your bedtime?"

"Didn't you hear?" the bully spat back. "School's canceled for the rest of the week! Turns out our principal's a member of that nerd-fest M.E.G.A.!"

"You out hunting for the alien, *Super-Sammi?*" Adriana Catalina sneered.

"*ACTUALLY, NO.*" A deep voice croaked, "*I WAS OUT HUNTING HER.*"

The middle school gang looked up in horror as a giant blobby shadow rose from the garbage bin behind Sammi. "*SHE SLAYED MY EVIL COMRADES ON THE PLANET, ER, MARIONNA, AND NOW I MUST HAVE MY VENGEANCE UPON HER! MWA-HAHAHAHAHA!*"

Sammi peered closely at him and was surprised to see the G'Dalien give her a wink. Moose and his gang stood frozen with their bikes, staring in horror as this enormous squidlike creature stepped out of his trash-bed and into the light of a streetlamp. "*NOW PREPARE TO WATCH ME EAT YOUR FRIENDS, ALIENSLAYER!*"

"Oh, they're not my friends," Sammi said casually. "Bon appétit."

A tiny squeal emitted from Moose's open mouth as the others attempted to flee. In their panic, they tangled their bikes into one another and fell over. As GOR-DON towered over the frigid bully, Moose shot his gaze at Sammi.

"Puh-puh-pleeeze . . ."

"Sorry, what was that?" Sammi said, cupping a

hand over her ear.

"...*h-h-help...*?"

"Oh, all right, just this once." Sammi exhaled. She turned to GOR-DON, who shrugged at her a tiny bit. She smiled, then charged him—diving onto his blubbery belly. GOR-DON let out an overly dramatic yell as he fell backward and let Sammi pretend to pummel him with fake punches and karate chops.

"AAAAARRRRGGGGH!" he yelled, really over-selling it. *"DANG YOU, ALIENSLAYER! YOU HAVE DEFEATED ME YET AGAIN! AAAARRRRGGGGHH!"*

In the confusion, Moose, Adriana, and the others collected their wits, climbed back onto their bikes, and sped off in different directions. Once the coast was clear, Sammi rolled off GOR-DON's belly. She was laughing harder than she had in days. He was laughing—well, maybe for the first time.

"*That* was fun," she said. "Why'd you help me?"

GOR-DON caught himself and stopped laughing. "I didn't do that to help you, *human*," he said, covering. "I just thought a bit of terrorizing might do me some good."

Sammi gave him a disbelieving look then suddenly remembered something. *THWACK!* She flicked him between the eyes.

"*Ow!*" GOR-DON said, looking at her. "That hurt, you vile ape!"

"That's for running away!" Sammi said. "Now tell me what's happening on the other end of that wormhole! Are Alex and Herbert in danger?"

"I honestly don't know," he said. "All I was told was to get you three to go try and save the future. AeroStar was waiting, but I have no idea what she had planned."

"This is bad. We've got to do something. I should've gone with them."

"Yeah, good thinking. Then she'd have all three of you."

THWACK! Sammi flicked him on the chin.

"*Ow!* Sweet screaming Plorgon!"

RUMBLE . . . The distant sound was like thunder

but different than thunder in that Sammi could not only hear it, she could feel it—under her feet. Like a baby earthquake.

RUMBLE . . . This time it set off the car alarm of a nearby minivan. "Uh-oh," GOR-DON said. "They're sprouting early. That's not good."

"Sprouting? What's sprouting? Your alien podseeds? *What have you done?*"

RUMBLE . . . GOR-DON shot her a worried look. "C'mon. We'd better get off the streets," he said.

AeroStar paced back and forth in front of the fake mouth of the fake cave on the wall of the fake caveman diorama, followed closely by a few MinionBots. For a headstrong evil queen, she seemed conflicted.

She suddenly stopped pacing, causing the MinionBots to bump and crash into one another. She screamed at the top of her lungs: "SARCASMA-CLEMCORP-A-TRON!"

A whirring, rolling sound came from down the long Hallway of Human History. AeroStar stepped over to the diorama railing and tapped her boot impatiently as the sound got louder.

"You shrieked, your *Humongousness*," a dry voice spoke from a long dining-room-table-size supercomputer. This incredibly intelligent machine built by Old Man Herbert had been used by the AlienSlayers but now had somehow found its way into the hands of their enemy. It had been given a slightly new name yet hadn't lost a drop of its smart-alecky attitude. "What's the problem? Having *too good* a day, O Evil One?"

"Where have you been?" she barked. "I didn't rescue you from a Dumpster and have you repaired, reprogrammed, and renamed just so you could lie around in sleep mode all day."

"Of course, your Giant-headedness," the machine said.

She held up a glowing clear-glass clipboard. "It's my Three-and-a-Half-Point Plan of Vengeance," she whined. "It's not going as cruelly as I'd imagined."

"I hate it when that happens," the sassy computer said, opening a small narrow slot on its console. "Hit me."

She inserted her glowing glass clipboard into

the slot and Sarcasma-ClemCorp-A-Tron beamed the contents of her concern into the air above them.

3½-POINT PLAN OF VENGEANCE AGAINST EXTREMELY IRRITATING ALIENSLAYERS (FINAL DRAFT)

☑ 1. HERBERT *(BRAINY, SCIENCE-LOVING NERD)*: DESTROY ALL G'DALIEN TECHNOLOGY, LEAVE HIM STRANDED FOREVER IN A WORLD DEVOID OF ANY COOL SCIENCE.

☑ 2. ALEX *(HEROIC, ADVENTURE-LOVING DIMWIT)*: EXILE SIDEKICK INTO SPACE ALONG WITH HELPLESS G'DALIENS, LEAVE HIM STRANDED FOREVER WITH NO WAY TO EVER SAVE THEM.

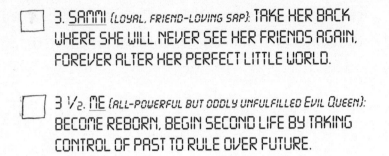

3. SAMMI *(LOYAL, FRIEND-LOVING SAP)*: TAKE HER BACK WHERE SHE WILL NEVER SEE HER FRIENDS AGAIN, FOREVER ALTER HER PERFECT LITTLE WORLD.

3 ½. ME *(ALL-POWERFUL BUT ODDLY UNFULFILLED EVIL QUEEN)*: BECOME REBORN, BEGIN SECOND LIFE BY TAKING CONTROL OF PAST TO RULE OVER FUTURE.

"Hey, two outta three and a half," Sarcasma-ClemCorp-A-Tron said. "Somebody's been a busy li'l Queen Bee. Keep up the bad work. Can I go now?"

"No!" AeroStar seethed. "The last item and a half are the most crucial points, and I'm unable to see them through! Sammi still needs to come here, see her friends in misery, and then travel back through the wormhole with me! It's all wrong!"

"This doesn't compute, my Hugeness. You have the suits. You have the wormhole. You have two of the three AlienSlayers where you want them. Just go and retrieve her, let her see your wickedness, then bring her back."

"*Are you overdue for an upgrade, you glorified workbench? THINK! The transformation works each time you pass through! I'll never achieve point three* and a half if my first pass with her is to *that* side of the wormhole! I've thought it through, back and forth, forth and back. If I start at her end, it doesn't work!"

Sarcasma-ClemCorp-A-Tron whirred, clicked, and buzzed, calculating at lightning speed before finally coming to a shocking conclusion. "Bless my motherboard. *You're right.* Perhaps I *am* overdue for an upgrade. . . ."

"Ugh . . . why am I surrounded by morons?"

"Couldn't you just go through the wormhole, find her, push her through, and then follow her, so you're not traveling together?"

"She'd find a way to avoid being recaptured. She may be misguided, but she's smart, fast, and crafty. She gets it from me."

As the supercomputer processed this new information, a whooshing sound caught both their attention. A MinionBot came zooming into the caveman diorama with the netted Alex and Herbert in tow. It released them, landed, and saluted its maker.

"Successfully seized and captured, my queen," the bot reported.

Alex and Herbert stood up and faced AeroStar. *Whizz-click!* A pair of laser blasters popped out of her tiara and pointed directly at each of them.

"Hey!" Herbert noticed the giant computer from their old SlayerLair.

"What are *you* doing here?" Alex asked.

"Never mind *him*," AeroStar said. "He works for me now."

"I hope you choke on one of his *horrible* smoothies," Alex said, remembering the incredibly delicious, not-horrible-at-all Mega-Choco-Bomb Marshmallow Root Beer Smoothies that Sarcasma-ClemCorp-A-Tron (then known as just SarcasmaTron) used to whip up for him.

"Unlikely," AeroStar sneered. "I'm lactose intolerant. *I WILL NOT TOLERATE LACTOSE.* In any case, I assume you saw the fates I've created for each of you out there. *Enjoy your stay! HAHAHA!*"

"You destroyed everything," Herbert said. "But it can all be rebuilt."

"*HA!* By whom? You and that washed-up old fart of a scientist version of you? Good luck to the both of you losers—especially with no G'Daliens to help you!"

"That genius inventor is gone," Herbert said. "But not in vain."

"Tell us where they are, you *hag*," Alex said through gritted teeth. "Where did you send Old Man Alex and my G'Dalien friends?"

"*Oh, if only I knew . . . ,*" AeroStar said in a mockingly sweet voice, then barking: "*I'D NEVER TELL YOU! HAHAHAHA!*" She stopped short and looked around at the MinionBots standing idly by. "*Ahem.* That was a *joke*, you idiots."

"Ha. Ha. Ha. Ha. Ha. Ha." The bots jerkily emitted forced, monotone laughter. She rolled her eyes at them and turned back to her captives.

"You may have gotten rid of Old Man Alex and

Old Man Herbert," Alex said. "But you still lose." He narrowed his eyes at her. "Because you'll never get Sammi."

"You don't know what you're talking about," AeroStar spat, glancing nervously over at Sarcasma-ClemCorp-A-Tron.

"You can do whatever you want to us," Herbert added. "We'll protect her until our last breath. Because she's our friend." The two ex-AlienSlayers shared a look and nodded in agreement.

AeroStar stared at the two of them standing defiantly before her. "*Hmm*," she purred. "What do you say we test that theory, shall we, *science boy?*"

A small beam of light shot from the center of her tiara and hit the clump of sewn-together N.E.D. suits, lifting them off the woolly mammoth tusks. "Sarcasma-ClemCorp-A-Tron," she said, "take these and dismantle them at once. I want them reconfigured into three original human-sized suits."

A panel slid open on one end of its mainframe, and AeroStar dropped the silver clump of material inside. "Ooh, sewing?" Sarcasma-ClemCorp-A-Tron snarked. "This is gonna be a real gigabyte-strainer."

RUMBLE The distant, baby earthquakes seemed to be getting stronger as Sammi sat across from GOR-DON in the town house.

"Alien pod-plants," she said. "Start talking."

The large creature sighed heavily. "It had nothing to do with AeroStar or her plans for you. The pod-planting was my idea. For years all I've done is execute evil plans for *her*—I figured I was entitled to a little . . . *me time*."

"Most people take a vacation," Sammi said. "Just so you know. But go on."

"The night I arrived, I snuck out and located an area with hospitable conditions for maximum gestation and initialized alien-to-soil implantation."

Sammi stared at him. He sighed. "I planted alien seeds. From the future."

"*What?*" Sammi's mind was reeling. "What kind of seeds?"

"Audreenian Non-Carnivorous Podling seeds," GOR-DON said, somewhat guiltily. "Stanky little things, too. Still can't get the smell off my claws." He sniffed his tiny fingers with a look of annoyance.

RUMBLE . . .

"Wait," Sammi said. "If they're just *podlings*, what's with all the rumbling? Podling means small no matter where you're from! What're we talking, knee high?"

"*HAW!*" GOR-DON burst out laughing. "Have you *been* to Audreenia? Yeah, knee-high to an Audreenian pod-farmer, who are *giants*! Audreenia's the biggest planet in the universe! Everything's HUGE there! You visit Audreenia and pick up a triple-extra petite-sized 'I ♥ AUDREENIA' T-shirt? You could fit it over a Truitillion carbon atomizer. We're talking big."

"You planted them in the Merwinsville Community Gardens!" Sammi said, putting everything together. "That's how the M.E.G.A. members got your picture."

"Not my best side, by the way. Made me look fat—"

"*Hey!*" Sammi kicked GOR-DON in the shin, or where his shin would be if tentacles had shins. Not too hard, but it got his attention. She stared at him sternly. "This is *my planet!* You can't just come here and plant Auditory Neo-carnito Potted . . ."

"Audreenian Non-Carnivorous Podling Plants," GOR-DON corrected her.

RUMBLE . . .

"Okay. So they're big. I get it. But you did say *non-*carnivorous, right?"

"Oh, yeah, yeah," GOR-DON reassured her. "They won't eat meat. Have no appetite for it. Unless they smell it, of course. The faintest whiff of meat turns them *extremely* carnivorous."

"So we make sure they don't smell meat. Got it. Do they even have noses?"

"Of course not. Plants don't have *noses*." Sammi breathed a sigh of relief—until he went on. "Their entire bodies are made up of olfactory cells, stalk to stem. They can smell the fart of a Boramian dust mite a mile away. Quite remarkable."

RUMBLE...

Sammi kicked GOR-DON again. Same place, only harder.

"Ow!"

"Why would you do this?"

GOR-DON slithered to his feet and stood before her. "For Marion, okay? I figured, maybe if I grew the podlings, I could destroy them. Or at least control them. Humans would think I was some sort of hero. Then I'd go back and bring Marion here and show her I wasn't such a . . . vile and disgusting loser."

Sammi stared at this sad, lonely, vulnerable,

misunderstood creature. She took a step toward him—and kicked him again, as hard as she could.

"Owee! Will you stop doing that?"

"That's the *lamest* plan I've ever heard! You know nothing about girls! What were you thinking?"

GOR-DON plopped back down in a lump. "I don't know. I messed up. Again."

"Yeah, kinda!"

GOR-DON buried his face in his tentacles and went to a very dark place. Sammi stared out at the night sky, trying to think of what to do.

RUUUUMMMMMMMMBLE . . .

It was the biggest one yet, and it came thundering loudly from the direction of the Merwinsville Park. Sammi turned around and faced GOR-DON. He was already standing up. They both had the same thought.

"Oh, no," Sammi said. *"Alex's family."*

Outside, in the Filbys' driveway, Sammi stood behind GOR-DON as he lifted the garage door with one of his tentacles. Sammi walked up to a large covered object. Yanking the cover off, even GOR-DON gasped. Sitting there, spotless and magnificent, its insectlike bubble window gleaming in the moonlight, was an avocado green AMC Pacer: Mr. Filby's prized possession. "I know I don't deserve it given what I've done," GOR-DON said. "But I'm *so* driving this transport vehicle."

Sammi opened the driver's-side door for him.

LET'S ROLL.

Floating helplessly above a violent thresher machine, Herbert stared down at a horrifying set of thrashing metal teeth.

"Why is it always me who ends up dangling over highly efficient delivery systems of grisly death?" he asked the stuffed woolly mammoth in the corner. It had no answer for him. "At least this one won't drool all over me before it tries to eat me alive." He sighed.

It was true. The clunky ClemCorp CityCrusher 3000 had a gaping mouth filled with rusty, pointed teeth, able to grind to rubble entire buildings made of iron, steel, and concrete. But unlike a Klapthorian Death Slug, it wasn't a drooler. So that was good.

Its rotating mouth, which housed the churning teeth, was turned straight up beneath Herbert, who was suspended by some sort of force field beam being projected by *another* strange machine, the ClemCorp BoulderMover X-10. This shot out a beam of energy designed to lift and move objects much larger and heavier than a twelve-year-old budding scientific genius. Wired to and sitting atop this piece of equipment was a much smaller device, labeled the ClemCorp BioScanner-L7. This had an electric eye that aimed its gaze at the fake mouth of the fake cave. It also showed a digital time display set for 60:00:00. The scanner's eye stared unblinkingly at what would soon be an open wormhole.

Alex finished zipping up his N.E.D. suit and took in all of these devices. *Well, this is quite a pickle*, he thought.

"Okay, listen up," AeroStar said. "I know you're not the smart one, but this is simpler than it looks, even for you. The holding beam will suspend your brainy friend above certain death for exactly sixty minutes. That's how much time you have to go through the wormhole, fetch Sammi, and bring her back to me. The BioScanner is set to identify her when she comes through. I know you have a history of playing dress-up. Do *not* try to fool BioScanner. If anyone but Sammi comes through that wormhole, the beam cuts out and science boy ends up looking like one of his failed experiments. And by that I mean he'll be crushed into a sort of gooey paste."

She tossed Alex the second of the three N.E.D. suits. "This is for her. Once she's through and gets BioScanned, it'll be safe for you to come back through. If you don't, I'll see to it that *both* of your friends get ground up. Get it? Got it? *Good.*"

Alex's mind was racing. He noticed something going on behind AeroStar, who was now fiddling with the BioScanner projector. The MinionBot that had caught them had inched its way over to Sarcasma-ClemCorp-A-Tron, extended a small connector device, and plugged it into the giant computer. Alex figured whatever it was doing, it might need more time. Thinking fast, he took a

step toward the ClemCorp CityCrusher 3000. "This is *cool*. I thought you got rid of all the G'Dalien technology."

"*Excuse me?*" AeroStar stepped toward him. "The 3000 is *not* a G'Dalien product. Those space squid *wished* they could create something as loud and violent as this."

"That's true," Alex whispered. "Between you and me, it always bothered me how peaceful and quiet the G'Dalien inventions were. *So boring.*"

She looked at him. "Are you mocking me? Because I will not be mocked."

Alex edged over to the BoulderMover. "And this—*genius*! So the G'Daliens nailed antigravity technology. *Big deal.* Give me a good old-fashioned, human-style energy-blasting holding ray any day."

As AeroStar squinted at him suspiciously, Alex grinned at her, keeping her attention away from the MinionBot attached to Sarcasma-ClemCorp-A-

Tron behind her. He nodded enthusiastically as she explained her creative process.

Meanwhile, inside the bot, Old Man Herbert sat cramped in his tiny airchair control hull. Pressing tiny knobs and buttons, he busily worked to access Sarcasma-ClemCorp-A-Tron's hard drive and memory system, overriding the megacomputer he himself had built, in search of some very important information. When a small screen lit up, so did his smile. "*Eureka!*" he whispered.

"All right, enough of this!" AeroStar had just finished her spiteful tale of how the G'Daliens and their technology had run her company into the ground and sent her into exile. "You've stalled long enough. *It's time.*"

Alex glanced over at Sarcasma-ClemCorp-A-Tron. The MinionBot had blended into a group of identical MinionBots standing in a clueless clump by the stuffed woolly mammoth. Alex tried not to panic. What was going on? What was he supposed to do? AeroStar stepped up to him menacingly. He put his hand on his N.E.D. suit switch, not at all sure what his next move should be.

"Excuse me, Caped Conqueror," a tinny voice called out. Alex stopped. He and AeroStar both looked up to see a MinionBot approach. It extended a body sensor and quickly scanned Alex's belly. "My readings indicate the human is dehydrated."

"So?" AeroStar said impatiently. "What's that got to do with anything?"

"It seems to me that if he were to pass out while in transit or when he reaches the other end of the wormhole, it could negatively affect the outcome of your otherwise ingenious Three-and-a-Half-Point Plan of Vengeance."

AeroStar rolled her eyes and looked at Alex. "Well? Is Dr. Clunky here right in his diagnosis? *Are you thirsty?*" Alex glanced at the MinionBot and tried to think fast—something that didn't come naturally to him. He shrugged. "Uh, yeah. Sure. I wouldn't mind a little something for the road."

AeroStar stomped her boot and looked around. There was nothing. Then she got an evil smile on her face. "Oh, I know. Those *horrible* smoothies you mentioned. The ones you used to get from *my* supercomputer. Drink one of those."

Alex glanced over at the MinionBot. Its electronic eye winked at him. He hid his smile by covering his face with his hands.

"*Noooo!*" Alex dropped to his knees and cried out dramatically, doing what he considered some of his best acting since he played Shrub #3 in his second grade class play. "*Anything* but one of that computer's Mega-Choco-Bomb Marshmallow Root Beer Smoothies! Have mercy, you—you *monster!*"

AeroStar smiled at his fake misery, then turned as she heard a soft *ding!* A small panel slid open and a frosty mug of slushy, brown liquid popped out. She chuckled in a sinister way as she presented the smoothie to Alex, who was mock-trembling in fear. Her tiara blasters clicked out and aimed at him as she thrust it in his face. "*Drink up.*" She grinned.

Alex took the mug and slowly raised the straw to his lips. *Sllllluuuuuurrrrp!* He drained it in two seconds, then topped it off with another sound effect. "*BUUUURRRRRRP!*"

Secretly, inside his mouth, Alex's tongue was

doing joyful somersaults. Of all the things he missed about Future Merwinsville, he'd completely forgotten how ridiculously delicious Mega-Choco-Bomb Marshmallow Root Beer Smoothies were.

On the outside, he dropped the mug, grabbed his head, and dropped to his knees as AeroStar happily looked on. The strange thing was *he wasn't faking.* A strange bolt of discomfort ran from his belly up his spine and into his brain. At first he thought this was a wicked case of brain freeze from slurping down the frozen drink. But Alex knew all too well what an ice cream headache felt like. This was very, very different. Like something surging from his belly, filling his brain.

"On your feet," AeroStar said. "You've stalled long enough; you've had your drink. Now it's time to go to work."

He stood up and looked at her. His mind felt foggy, like he was trying to remember something he'd forgotten. Suddenly, the fog began to lift—in fact, things became incredibly clear. In his mind's eye he could see a list of instructions, as clearly as if they were written right in front of him. He shook his head and they jiggled out of view. He saw AeroStar step to

the BioScanner and start the clock. The digital timer began counting down: *60:00, 59:59, 59:58, 59:57 . . .*

"Tick-tock, *minion*," she said. "Better get a move on, and remember, *NO TRICKS!*"

The list kept popping up in Alex's mind, and he kept shaking it away. He cleared his head long enough to locate the switch to his N.E.D. suit, and he flipped it.

WUBBA-WUBBA-WUBBA-WUBBA! The wormhole portal shimmered to life and tugged Alex toward it. Shaking the strange list of instructions out of his brain one more time, he glanced up at Herbert, then took two steps and leaped through the portal.

CHAPTER 19

UH OH.

CHAPTER
20

*P*OP! Alex shot out of the sticker mirror on the wall of the *Fluffy Stuff 'n' Pals Teaparty Townhouse* and landed in a pile of stuffed animals. He got up and looked around. The plastic two-story dollhouse was dark and silent. He ran down the spiral staircase, out onto the lawn, and into his house.

"*Hello?*" Alex ran into the kitchen. Something wasn't right. The instruction list popped into his head again and he shook it off. "Quit it, you stupid brain!"

SCREEECH! The sound of tires squealing startled him. He burst out the front door just in time to see his father's prized AMC Pacer peel out of the driveway and barrel down the street, zigging and zagging all the way to the end of the block. It fishtailed around the corner and disappeared. Alex's father loved that car. He worshipped that car. He never let the tires of that car touch the street, never mind lay down skid marks halfway down his block. Something was *really* not right.

As he walked back inside, the instruction list popped up in his mind's eye again. This time, standing alone in his dark house, he decided not to shake it away. He closed his eyes, focused on it, and began reading.

PARALLEL UNIVERSE PERSPECTIVE ENHANCER (P.U.P.E.)
ASSEMBLY INSTRUCTIONS

1. LOCATE AND OPEN INTERNAL TRANSMITTER BOARD ON BACK OF HELMET.

2. INSIDE, FIND AND ATTACH MAIN RECEIVER WIRE TO ANTENNAE INPUT JACK.

3.

SPLICE OUTGOING ANTENNAE
SIGNAL INDICATOR WIRE TO
BOTH FRONTAL- AND REAR-LOBE
TRANSMITTER POSTS.

4.
FIBER-OPTIC THREADS SHOULD
RUN FROM NEURAL TRANSMITTER
POSTS INTO HELMET'S INNER SHELL,
THEN CONNECT TO CONTACT SENSORS.
CHECK EACH CONNECTION, AND SEE
THAT ALL SENSORS ARE EVENLY
DISTRIBUTED INSIDE HELMET.

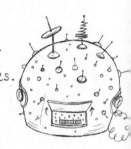

5.

LOCATE RETINAE AND PROJECTION
COORDINATE INDICATORS SOME-
WHERE INSIDE VISOR SCREEN AND
TRANSMITTER BOARD, RESPECTIVELY.
CALIBRATE BOTH TO "20122122."

Alex opened his eyes. "That crazy old genius! He must've swiped the instructions from SarcasmaTron's hard drive *and downloaded them into my Mega-Choco-Bomb Marshmallow Root Beer Smoothie!*" Alex shut his eyes again and giggled as he scrolled through the rest of the instructions. There were at least fifty rather complicated steps. With the detail and precision each required, factoring in the limited amount of supplies he'd have access to in Herbert's bedroom lab, he quickly calculated that in order to reassemble a working Parallel Universe Perspective Enhancer he would need—exactly thirty-eight point sixteen seconds. He opened his eyes again. "Whoa," he said. "I think I picked up a few extra gigglebytes of processing power, too. That was some smoothie."

With no time to spare, Alex ran out back, found Herbert's P.U.P.E. helmet, then bolted next door. *Ding-dong-VROOM!* Alex was already in a crouched position when the Slewgs' DoorSmell sniffer device sprung out at him. When Mrs. Slewg opened the door, she was surprised to see him.

"Hello, Alex! Is there anything wrong?" she said. "I hope my little Herbie's behaving himself over there."

"He sure is." Alex was speaking rapidly. He felt like his brain was ten steps ahead of his mouth. "And by 'over there' you obviously mean my house. Because that's where you assume he is. Which *is* where he is, assuming that's where you think he is. Which you do. Correct?"

"Uh, yes, of course! I'm so glad you two are having a sleepover tonight, what with all this alien nonsense. I mean, canceling school. *Honestly.*"

"No, no! He's having a great time! In fact, he's having so much fun, he didn't want to stop to come and get his toothbrush, toothpaste, pajamas, fresh underwear, clean clothes for the morning, and favorite pillow. So here I am, to help a friend."

She gave him an odd grin. "Alex," she said. "You don't have to lie to me. I know why you're really here." Alex froze. His choco-charged mind began to process the statistical probability of Mrs. Slewg actually being a mind-reading invention of Herbert's. He calculated it to be 17,426,832,694 to 1.

"He asked you to sneak up to his room to get his *lovey*, didn't he? He knows I think he's too old to sleep with that stuffed periodic table of the elements." She smiled at him. "You're a good friend.

Go on. He keeps 'Tabley' under his pillow. Thinks I don't know about it. *I'll pretend I didn't see you*," she whispered.

Alex forced a smile at her and nodded his thanks. He ran up the stairs, down the hall, and locked Herbert's bedroom door behind him.

Standing at Herbert's worktable, Alex shut his eyes and began following the first of the instructions. His Mega-Choco-Bombed brain knew just what the intricate steps meant, exactly which parts they referred to, and precisely the right tools needed to make new, missing components. With a rush he had never experienced before, Alex's hands were a blur as he set to work fixing the P.U.P.E. helmet. He grinned as he worked away at the invention. For the first time, he kind of understood Herbert's whole technology thing. He'd never admit it to Herbert, of course, but being smart felt pretty good.

Exactly thirty-eight-point sixteen seconds later, he set the helmet down and opened his eyes. As exciting as it was to finish the project, a sudden sinking feeling hit his belly. He was confident the helmet would work, but now came the hard part: having to look at whatever it showed him. The way it was designed, if the 111-year-old version of himself was somewhere in the future wearing the prototype he stole from Old Man Herbert, Alex would be able to see whatever his older, parallel universe self was looking at. And whatever that was might not be good.

Alex took a deep breath and flipped a switch. The helmet hummed to life, and a light on the side of it glowed red. He knew this meant there was no incoming signal. Hoping it was a glitch, he slipped the helmet on his head and dropped the black visor down over his eyes. Then he did something very unscientific. He crossed his fingers.

Everything was very dark. After a moment, Alex reached up to the control pad on the side of the helmet and flipped the switch on and off again. Nothing. Then a message appeared on the inside of the black visor that made him go cold.

He stared at the message, straining as hard as he could to send out brain waves through the helmet, hoping his new brainpower would boost the signal and his 111-year-old self would somehow pick up. When the screen went dark again, he finally took off the helmet and carried it out of Herbert's room.

Alex felt more alone and depressed than he ever had. But knew he had to snap out of it. He didn't have time to feel bad for himself. Time was running out. He jumped the hedge and ran into his backyard, looking for Sammi. He ran back into the tea party town house. Tossing the P.U.P.E. helmet on a pile of stuffed animals, he called out to her, but it was still deserted. A weird feeling crept over him—he didn't know what it meant, but he didn't like it.

RUUUUMMMMMMMBLE...

The baby earthquake shook the town house, causing him to stumble down the stairs. Alex ran to the front of the house and looked in the direction the rumbling seemed to have come from.

"The community gardens," he said to himself. Alex felt like he was in the middle of a crazy dream that was getting crazier by the second. There was something happening here that he knew wasn't right. He had to find Sammi, and he had to make sure his family was safe. Alex jumped on his bike and pointed it toward the source of the rumbling. He tried to put out of his mind the very real possibility that his good friend Old Man Alex was gone forever—and he headed for the park.

"The tension is deliciously unbearable." AeroStar grinned, pacing between the booby-trapped fake cave entrance and the line of MinionBots.

"Try waiting it out from where I'm sitting," Herbert said from high above the threshing steel teeth of the CityCrusher 3000.

"*SILENCE!*" AeroStar barked up at him. "Or you will feel even more of my wrath."

Despite his predicament, Herbert chuckled at this. "I'm suspended by a beam of light over a chomping death machine, hoping *Alex Filby* comes through for me. What more could you possibly do?"

She was about to show him when suddenly Sarcasma-ClemCorp-A-Tron began to go berserk. Which really wasn't his style.

"MEMORY BREACH! MEMORY BREACH!" Alarms and sirens began going off all over the table-sized supercomputer's terminal. *"EEEEEK! I'VE BEEN VIOLATED!"*

AeroStar spun around and noticed a wire dangling from the supercomputer's side terminal. She followed it to where the other end lay, in front of the line of MinionBots. "A-HA!" she said, pointing her tiara cannons at the line of identical bots. "So our imposter has foolishly returned." She looked each one over carefully. "One of you is that pathetic old scientist, the elder version of the pathetic *young* scientist dangling overhead. I trust the only reason you're here is to rescue him, so I will give you that opportunity now." She stepped back and stood near the BoulderMover, which held Herbert overhead. "I will count to three. If you do not step forward and identify yourself, I will drop the young Slewg into the crusher."

She scanned the two rows of bots carefully to see if any of them made a move. *"One . . . two . . . thr—"* *CLANG!* A MinionBot in the front line stumbled forward awkwardly. AeroStar pounced forward, engaged her cannon, and fired. *PHZZZZATT!* In an instant the bot was blown to pieces.

"No!" Herbert yelled from above—until he saw the two halves of the bot's exposed wires, mechanics, and other clunky junk one would expect to see fall out of a split-open MinionBot. At the sight of one of their fellow minions brutally slain, the other bots defaulted into panic mode.

They spun in circles and clanged into one another as AeroStar fumed. "*A TRICK!*" she screamed, and began blasting randomly at the scurrying bots like fish in a barrel. Chunks of bots were flying around the smoke-filled room, making it difficult to see. Fed up, AeroStar finally lunged for the kill switch to the BoulderMover. "*Wherever you are, you can say good-bye to your nerdy little friend!*" she shrieked.

She slammed the button just as a large hunk of blasted MinionBot came hurtling from the scrap heap. It slammed the BoulderMover's cannon, jerking the beam violently. As it shifted, it cut out, sending Herbert flying. Instead of falling into the grinding teeth of the CityCrusher, he slammed sideways into the stuffed woolly mammoth.

"*Oof!*" He hit the mammoth with a dull thud but grabbed onto its fur and scrambled up onto its back.

"*NOOOO!*" AeroStar blasted away at anything in her sight. MinionBots went flying, and the CityCrusher was obliterated. One last MinionBot sprang into the air from behind a pile of debris and morphed into Old Man Herbert's airchair. AeroStar opened fire on the old man, who expertly dodged her destructive blasts.

Herbert slid down the mammoth's forehead and off its trunk, snatching the last N.E.D. suit from the mammoth's tusk as he flew in the air. Old Man Herbert swooped down and caught him, and together they zoomed over the scene: the charred walls of the diorama, the smoking hulk of the CityCrusher, the piles of blasted MinionBots, and finally the siren-blaring Sarcasma-ClemCorp-A-Tron. They buzzed AeroStar, forcing her to dive into the dirt, before zooming out into the Hallway of Human History, toward the museum lobby and the world outside.

"*MINIONBOTS! SEIZE THEM!*" AeroStar froze, then turned around, wondering why her orders were being disobeyed. Behind her, lying in a massive scrap heap, were what was left of her MinionBots, all of which she'd blasted to smithereens. "*Fine,*" she snapped at the lifeless metal husks. "I'll just have to do it myself."

Herbert closed his eyes and felt the wind in his face as he clung to the back of Old Man Herbert's chair. For a moment, he tried to forget that the city below him was now in ruins.

KA-BLAM! The airchair jolted violently, causing him to open his eyes, but also to lose his grip and nearly fall off. He scrambled to pull himself back on board. The airchair was sputtering, thrusting, and zigzagging like it had gone crazy. Old Man Herbert tried to control it, but it seemed to have a mind of its own.

KA-BLAM! It jerked again, and Herbert looked out to see what was happening. There was AeroStar, flying straight at them, powered by her smoke-belching Utility Tiara. The golden hairpiece was also shooting bright blasts of energy at them. *KA-FZZT!* A blast just missed them, only because the

malfunctioning chair suddenly jerked downward for no apparent reason. She was getting closer now, and Herbert could make out her evil smile as she approached.

"Get us on the ground!" Herbert yelled, looking down. Below them lay miles and miles of smashed buildings and roads, with more than a few MagnaWreckers grinding away on what was left of the city providing no soft landing spots.

"I'm trying, but it isn't responding!" Old Man Herbert yelled. He was madly hitting buttons and pushing levers on the console. The chair was now not only flying crazily, but large sections of it were shifting and moving, as if it couldn't make up its mind what to morph into. Herbert was having a very difficult time hanging on.

KA-FZZT! Another energy blast whizzed past them, winging the bottom of the chair. It caused the airchair to stop morphing, but it spun in midair, nearly knocking Old Man Herbert out of his seat. Herbert scrambled to help his elder self back in. Old Man Herbert couldn't get his airchair to do anything but hover—it was suspended by short spurts of its damaged booster jets.

Herbert looked around frantically for AeroStar. He froze when he saw her hovering in the sky directly in front of them, about fifty yards away. She was close enough so Herbert could see the tiny laser cannon on her Utility Tiara focused directly on them. Herbert glanced down—they were too far up to jump, and they were powerless to move. There was no way out. *This is it*, he thought.

POW! Seemingly out of nowhere, a large object— like a white, fluffy pillow of death—suddenly slammed into AeroStar from above, knocking her out of the sky and sending her plummeting like a stone.

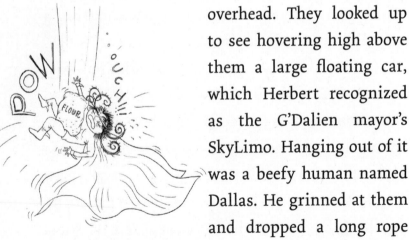

"*Hey! Up here!*" a familiar voice called out from overhead. They looked up to see hovering high above them a large floating car, which Herbert recognized as the G'Dalien mayor's SkyLimo. Hanging out of it was a beefy human named Dallas. He grinned at them and dropped a long rope ladder. Another boy with a baseball cap peeked out next to him. It was Chicago, sitting in the driver's seat.

Far below, AeroStar had hit the ground, but her Utility Tiara had shot out a spray of thick, gelatinous goo, which expanded like foam and broke her fall. She heaved the giant pillow from her lap and looked up to see Herbert helping Old Man Herbert out of his malfunctioning airchair and onto the ladder.

"*This is not over,*" she muttered angrily.

Herbert helped Old Man Herbert into the SkyLimo and quickly gave a series of hugs and high fives to his old friends Chicago, Dallas, and a skinny, buglike kid named Sausalito. There was little time for a reunion, however, and the burly Dallas quickly dragged another heavy pillow-bomb to the edge of the SkyLimo. Herbert saw it was a giant sack of flour. Printed on its side was a familiar logo, the name of the greatest pizza place in all the past, present, or future: ANDRETTI'S PIZZERIA.

"Okay, on three!" Dallas yelled. Herbert looked down and was shocked to see AeroStar zooming straight at them.

"Make it two!" Sausalito yelled to his beefy partner.

"Forget the count," Herbert hollered at both of them "Drop it! NOW!"

They hoisted the sack over the edge as AeroStar approached rapidly. POW! The sack hit her as before, but this time it smacked her in the head. The impact sent her falling in a tailspin, head over boots.

"Direct hit!" Old Man Herbert yelled.

"Now let's get out of here before she comes back," Chicago said. He put his foot to the floor, and a grinding blast of dirty smoke shot out the back of the SkyLimo. Herbert noticed that this wasn't quite the same smooth-running, antigravity, flying car that had once belonged to the G'Dalien mayor, but it was putting distance between him and AeroStar's Utility Tiara, so it would do just fine.

CHAPTER 2
RUMBLE RUMBLE RUMBLE

Alex weaved his bike through the hundreds of people crowding the streets of Merwinsville—some heading toward the community gardens, but many more running away from it.

He peered at the panicked faces, searching for his mom, dad, sister, or Sammi.

RUUMMMMBBLE . . . The ground shook beneath him again. "*Ellie!*" Alex yelled across the crowd as he rode directly toward the source of the noise. As he got closer to the Merwinsville Community Gardens, the crowd grew thicker. There was a strange feeling in the air, like something very bad was about to happen.

He pushed his way through to the garden walls and saw the members of both M.U.L.C.H. and M.E.G.A. surrounding and standing on it, staring into the garden, waiting. The M.E.G.A. members had their cameras and alien-detecting sensors pointed at a massive mound of dirt in the center of the garden. The M.U.L.C.H. members also stood at the ready, holding rakes, hoes, and weed wackers.

"Mom! Dad!" Alex yelled again, scanning the faces in the two groups, hoping to spot his parents.

"Alex! Over here!" His parents had Ellie and were standing on a clearing overlooking the garden. Alex ran to them, and together they turned to look out over the strange bump in the center of the garden.

RUUMMMMMBLLE . . . The mound suddenly shifted, shaking the earth beneath their feet. M.E.G.A. cameras whirred and clicked, the M.U.L.C.H. members lifted their gardening tools like weapons, and the crowd in general suddenly let out a collective gasp. A bud of something green and large sprouted out of the ground. Its leaves folded open like a blossoming flower, then bent back down and pushed off the surrounding mound like the arms of a person lifting himself out of a bathtub filled with dirt. The soil erupted in another massive rumble, and Alex and his family huddled together as they watched the giant head of the pod-plant emerge from the dirt like a zombie plant rising from the grave. Its long, sinewy stem then pushed its head ten, twenty, thirty, forty feet into the night sky.

Many people backed off and ran, but Alex stood his ground along with his mother, father, and little sister. The community groups also watched in awe as this strange plant grew taller and taller before their eyes. When it finally stopped growing, it was the height of a two-story building and stood swaying in the cool night air. For a brief moment, there was a confused but slightly relieved reaction from the crowd. It was a massive plant, yes—but it was still a *plant*. What could it do?

As if to answer that very question, the plant suddenly tossed its head back and let out a horribly loud, ear-piercing squeal: "*EEEEEEAAAAAAAHHHHHH!*"

Everyone covered their ears. The sounds of car

alarms and windows smashing from the incredibly high-pitched shrieking sound were heard nearby.

RUUUUUMMMMMMBLLLLLE! The ground shook and shifted again as the plant lifted its roots out of the soil, like a giant pulling its buried feet out of the mud. The ground covering the roots buckled so severely that the garden wall where many of the Merwinsvillians were standing cracked and crumbled, sending them tumbling off and falling to the ground. The plant lifted one of its rootlike legs high into the air and brought it down with a ground-shaking *THUD!* It did the same with the other leg, and soon was stomping through the garden. Its pod-mouth drew back and opened, emitting another unholy shriek.

"EEEEEEEEEEEAAAAAAAAAAAAHHHHHHHH!"

Alex and his parents joined the sudden frenzy of panic. Even the hard-core M.E.G.A. members were scrambling for shelter as the plant began to stomp slowly toward the park. *"Sammi!"* Alex yelled above the screams. He spotted her, alone and frightened, trying to fight her way against the flow of the mob.

Alex broke away from his family and struggled to reach her, pulling her out of the swarming crowd. She hugged him when she saw him. "We've got to get your family out of here," she said. "These things are *not* friendly."

"Where'd they come from?"

"I'll give you one fat, blobby guess."

"GOR-DON! Did he escape?"

"Er, not exactly. He actually *drove.* It's a long story."

"So where is he?"

"He's here. We came together to find your family but decided he should stay hidden from the crowd. We didn't want to cause a panic."

Alex looked around at the pandemonium. "Yeah, we wouldn't want to start a *riot* or anything. Wait— did you say *'we'*?"

WE?

"I told you, it's a long story." Mr. and Mrs. Filby suddenly broke through the crowd from behind the two of them, out of breath. Ellie was with them, too. She seemed to be enjoying this.

"C'mon," Sammi said. "This way. You've all got to trust me. This is going to get worse. There are more of them."

EEEEEEEAAAAA!

They all looked over at the garden and saw three more giant pod-plant creatures rise from behind the crumbled wall.

"This way! Quickly!"

The Filby family followed as Sammi led them through the woods and into a clearing where Mr. Filby's prized slime green AMC Pacer sat gleaming in the moonlight, without a scratch on it.

Mr. Filby was confused at first, then panicked, then relieved to see that his car was in one piece, considering the mayhem that was going on nearby. Tears filled his eyes as he stepped forward and hugged its massive, bubblelike window. "Thank goodness! First my family and now my baby—all safe and sound!" He sobbed.

"EEEEEEEEEEEEAAAAAAAAAAAAAHHHHHHHHH!"

SMASH! The bubble-dome window on Mr. Filby's AMC Pacer exploded from the high-pitched squelch. As the others dived into the woods at the sight of a pod-plant creature looming over the treetops just above them, Mr. Filby turned and blocked his car with his body, defying the trunk-footed creature.

"Daryl, no!" cried Mrs. Filby. She tried to get up to move toward him, but Alex held her back. As the alien creature lifted its giant craggy root-foot above Mr. Filby and his Pacer, GOR-DON suddenly leaped out from behind a nearby bush and knocked

Mr. Filby to the ground. The two of them rolled away, and Mr. Filby looked back to see a pod-plant creature's root-foot crash down on the car with a horrible *CRUNCH!*

Mr. Filby threw his head back and screamed into the night sky as the pod-plant creature shook the car off its foot like a tin can.

"NOOOOOOOOOOO!"

Chicago landed the SkyLimo on the roof of Andretti's Pizzeria, one of the few buildings left standing in all of Future Merwinsville. Herbert was glad to see the old historic pizza place and was thankful that it had been spared. Andretti's was one of the Future Merwinsville's rare non-G'Dalien structures.

They scrambled out of the SkyLimo and quickly covered it with a tarp that exactly matched the roof of the building, camouflaging it from above. Then they ran into the stairwell, carrying Old Man

Herbert down the steps and into the boarded-up inside dining area of Andretti's Pizzeria.

Where humans and G'Daliens had once floated around eating delicious pizza in antigravity bumper booths there was now a large empty, dusty floor. In the center was a big table cluttered with pizza boxes and half-eaten pizzas. There was also a giant map of Merwinsville on the wall, with little red lights marking the current locations of all the ClemCorp MagnaWreckers. Stacked against the walls were big sacks of flour like the one that had taken out AeroStar.

"Welcome to Andretti's Underground Pizza Delivery Service," Chicago said.

"And laboratory," Old Man Herbert said from his old airchair; he sat hovering before the makeshift computerized map. He was fiddling with some buttons and switches, monitoring the wreckers. "Since the city was destroyed and the G'Daliens exiled, humans have had a hard time fending for themselves. They'd gotten pretty used to having everything come easy."

Chicago stepped over to a wood-burning oven behind the old counter bar. "We learned how to make pizzas the old-fashioned way and worked out an underground delivery network to get people fed." Herbert looked inside the small brick oven. Yummy-looking cheese and pepperoni pizzas were crisping up nicely. Tending to it in a large apron was Chicago's dad, Mr. Illinois. The tough old harmony enforcement cop looked a little silly in an apron.

"Hello, sir," Herbert said respectfully.

Mr. Illinois grinned strangely and didn't seem to recognize Herbert. "Hungry? What toppings would you like? We've got pepperoni, sausage, linguica . . ." He trailed off.

Herbert looked at Chicago. "Dad hasn't been the same since his partner, LO-PEZ, disappeared with the other G'Daliens," Chicago whispered. "He just makes pizzas all day. I'm kind of worried about him." Herbert watched as the once-gruff security guard turned back to the oven with his giant oversize spatula and slid a hot pizza onto the counter.

"So we deliver pizzas to people through underground tunnels," Dallas said.

"But for the places our underground tunnels can't reach, we've got this bad boy," Sausalito added. He pulled a tarp off what had once been the back wall of the restaurant, now just a crude, blasted-open hole leading to the outside. Parked there was an old tank, complete with treads, turret, and what looked like a massive water cannon mounted on top. "It's the official Andretti's Pizza Delivery Tank—it even has a root beer cannon!"

"Thirty minutes or less; it's hot or it's free," Mr. Illinois added proudly.

"Dad. It's always free." Chicago said gently.

"Right. I forgot."

Herbert scanned the room and took in the

desperate outpost of these rebels. They stared at him, waiting for a response. He hopped up onto the counter. "Listen, you guys. I know how bad it's been for you all here, how much you miss your G'Dalien friends, how much suffering you've seen since AeroStar did this."

"Down with AeroStar!" Sausalito yelled. The others cheered in response.

"She's an awful, awful person," Herbert continued. "But all of this pain and destruction she's caused, it's partly the fault of your AlienSlayers. Alex, Sammi, and I didn't know it at the time, but we crossed AeroStar. And her Plan of Vengeance included destroying the city—and shipping the G'Daliens off. So I just want to say I'm sorry. But I also want to say that together *we're going to make things right again!"*

The room lit up in cheers and high fives. Herbert grinned as he looked down on his ragtag little team. For the first time, he kind of got Alex's whole adventure thing. He'd never admit it to Alex, of course, but being heroic felt pretty good.

"Listen up! Alex is back in my world right now, trying to figure out the whereabouts of the S.S.

Clemtanic. It's a ridiculously improbable long shot, but if anyone's good at delivering ridiculously improbable long shots, it's Alex."

They cheered again. "What can we do to help?" Chicago asked.

"Either he or Sammi will be coming back through the wormhole. And when they do, AeroStar will be waiting for them. We need to clear that entry point. Any chance one of your underground pizza delivery tunnels leads to the Museum of Human History?"

Chicago shared a quick smile with Dallas and Sausalito. "Thirty minutes or less," he said.

Ellie and her parents sat in the Filby living room, still shaking from their experience. Sitting across from them was GOR-DON, slumped in a recliner, smiling awkwardly. Laid out in front of them, completely untouched, was a plate of chocolate-chip cookies. There was a long silence, then Mr. Filby turned to his wife.

"Well?"

"Not now, Daryl."

"Say it."

"I was wrong about the aliens, and your little welcoming group was right."

"And?"

She shot him another look, then forced a smile over at GOR-DON. *"And I'd like to welcome you to our home."*

Standing inside the *Fluffy Stuff 'n' Pals Teaparty Townhouse*, Alex's computer-smoothie-upgraded brain was still racing as he told Sammi how bad things were in Future Merwinsville. He found he was able to keep a clock in the back of his mind, *to the second*, even as he spoke to her. This meant he also knew he was close to running out of time. And every few minutes he was interrupted by the distant noise of an alien pod-plant smashing something.

"But how?" Sammi said in disbelief. "How can *all the G'Daliens be gone?*"

"AeroStar," he said. "She's very real. And very sneaky. She tricked them and shipped them off. Old Man Alex, too. I came back to repair Herbert's Parallel Universe Perspective Enhancer, then use it to observe through Old Man Alex's eyes his immediate surroundings, thereby allowing me to hypothesize an imprecise estimate that might lead me to pinpoint his logistical bearings."

Sammi stared at him. "Um, what?"

"Sorry. I drank a computer-enhanced Mega-Choco-Bomb Marshmallow Root Beer Smoothie, which internally downloaded directly to my brain instructions on how to fix Herbert's malfunctioning P.U.P.E. device. Evidently, the informational transfer seems to have stimulated the processing capacity of my cerebral cortex. Kind of a long story."

"Longer than *that*?"

"It doesn't matter now. There was no one on the other end of the P.U.P.E. I'm afraid Old Man Alex—and the G'Daliens—are gone, and there's no way to locate them. It was a waste of time. Which reminds me, time's almost up. I have to get back, immediately."

"*Time's almost up?* Who's timing you? What's going on?"

Alex looked at her. Unfortunately, faster data processing didn't help in the breaking-of-horrible-news department. "It's complicated," he said. She stared at him, and he knew this wouldn't do. But he had to go. "Okay. This AeroStar, she booby-trapped the wormhole. Herbert's life is in danger, and unless you"—he quickly self-corrected—"er, I mean *I* come back within an hour, she'll likely grind him up into Herburger."

"*Oh, no—wait a minute,*" Sammi said suspiciously. "You said unless *I* come back. Does she want you to come back, or does she want me?"

Alex's mind quickly processed response possibilities like a computer stuck in a programming loop. There were no good options. He couldn't tell Sammi the truth because she'd leap into danger to save Herbert. But he couldn't save Herbert himself. If he did nothing, time would run out and Herbert would die anyway. As possible reactions flashed through his mind, each one dead-ended at the same horrible conclusion: Herbert would be crunched into bits. To make things worse, Alex was beginning to feel the effects of his super-brain smoothie fading. But Sammi was still staring at him. Time was slipping away. He had to say something. He opened his mouth. "Erp—" he said.

The smoothie was wearing off faster than he'd realized.

"Alex, what's going on? This AeroStar—*who is she?*"

Alex silently pleaded for his brain to work faster. He struggled to sort through the various consequences of answering *this* impossible question. He couldn't tell Sammi that the evil menace responsible *was her parallel universe self.* She would freak out, which wouldn't be helpful to anyone. But he couldn't lie to her because—well, because he *couldn't.* His brain was beginning to slow down. He was hungry. He liked cookies.

"*Alex! Who is she?*"

"Uh, well, she's got black hair, like yours. And she's kinda—*pretty.*"

Sammi looked at him like he was insane. "What are you talking about? Who cares if she's *pretty?* What are her powers?"

"Oh! I meant pretty . . . *powerful!* I didn't mean she's *pretty*-pretty! I mean, even if she looked *just like you*, she wouldn't be as pretty as you are, although if you were 111 years old, you might. Not that I'm saying you are now or she was then. Or you will be when you get to be her age or anything 'cause you're *not.* Her, I mean. Or she's you. Except, of course, she kinda is, and you—y'know, *are.*"

Sammi stared at Alex. In the distance, a car

alarm went off as an alien pod-plant crushed a midsize sedan.

"Alex. You're being weird, even for you. *I am what?*"

"Her." His brain finally deflated. He couldn't think anymore. It was too much work. He took a deep breath. "AeroStar is the 111-year-old version of you. She's Old Lady you. She's mean. She's awful. And it turns out she's the parallel-universe version of you." He slumped and exhaled as the last traces of the brain-smoothie faded away. "Wow. That is *such* a relief. Thinking is *way* overrated."

Sammi grabbed Alex by the arms and shook him.

"See? This is why I didn't want to tell you! I knew you'd freak out!"

Sammi let go of him. The anger in her face turned to confusion, then anger again, and finally settled on determination.

"Of course. That's why she wants me, not you."

"She wants all three of us. Something about a master plot of destiny or something. I'm supposed to get you to go through the wormhole so she can do her revenge on you. Then I follow so she can do some revenge on me. She's got us, Sammi. She wants us to walk right into her big mousetrap."

"What about Herbert?"

"He'd be the cheese."

"Give me the suit," Sammi said.

Alex stared at her for a moment, then held the extra suit behind his back. "No," he said. "Herbert and I don't agree on much, but we agreed on this one thing. We decided that no matter what happened to us—we'd keep you safe."

"Aww . . ." Sammi smiled. "That is the sweetest thing anyone's ever done for me." She leaned in slowly. Alex shut his eyes so she could kiss him on the cheek again.

She skipped the kiss and snatched the suit from him. "But sorry. I'm going through the wormhole."

"Sammi, you can't! You don't know her."

"I think it's time we met, don't you?"

"You said you didn't want to meet your older self! It'd be weird, remember?"

"You mean 'weird' like if you found out your older self was an evil, power-mad tyrant? That kind of 'weird'?" She looked at Alex, who was clearly conflicted, and more than a little concerned. "Listen, Alex. Your future self is cool. He's goofy, but he's cool. I look at him, I look at you, and he makes sense. Herbert's future self makes sense. You can see how they're each extensions of you guys. I just found out that my future self is a horrible person who destroyed her world and is bent on revenge against me and my best friends. I have to know why. I have to know how that happened. I have to—I have to make sure that she isn't what I'm going to become."

She studied his face. "Alex. Tell the truth. If it were you, what would you do?"

"If my future self were evil and trying to hurt my friends?" He thought for a moment, then stopped thinking. He smiled. "I'd track myself down and go Solo Libre on my butt."

She smiled back.

"But listen to me, Sammi. AeroStar was clear. If I don't come through a minute after you do, she'll destroy both you *and* Herbert."

"Well, then that gives me one minute to kick her butt, right?"

"*EEEEEEEEEEAAAAAAAAAAHHHHHH!*" Another terrifying pod-plant squeal echoed over the town.

"Besides," Sammi said, flipping the switch on her N.E.D. suit, "as much as I could use the help of Alex Filby, this town has a bit of an alien problem. It needs El Solo Libre. And even he can't be in two centuries at one time."

She gave him a quick smile then leaped. *FOOMPH!* A second later she was gone, and Alex was alone.

Mr. and Mrs. Filby sat on either side of a sobbing GOR-DON, who had joined them on the couch. Ellie was getting squished to the side and looked very annoyed.

"There, there," Mrs. Filby said, patting the G'Dalien's stubbly scalp. "I know it's rough losing someone you care about, but it gets better. You have to trust us."

"I'm hungry," Ellie said rudely. "Can we *please* get a pizza?"

"*SHHH!*" Both her parents shot her the same look at the same time. Ellie stomped her foot and stormed out of the room.

"I've been there, big guy," Mr. Filby said. "Before I met Alex's mom, I knew this girl. Her name was Brenda, and she was a cha-cha dancer. And I'm gonna just say it, because I feel like we're all being real here. *Brenda cha-cha'd away with my heart.*"

"*Daryl!*" Mrs. Filby smacked her husband, who quickly adjusted his story.

"Of course, looking back, not a day goes by when I don't thank my lucky stars she left me," he stammered, putting his arm around his wife stiffly. "Or I wouldn't have met this little gem here. Right, honey?"

As Mrs. Filby pulled away from her husband, GOR-DON sniffled and smiled at the two of them. "You two are so kind," he said. "I truly don't deserve any of this. I feel just awful about infecting your planet with giant man-eating alien pod-plants."

"The important thing," Mrs. Filby said, "is you learn to love yourself."

Mr. Filby smiled in agreement with his wife. "Yep. That's the key." He turned back to GOR-DON. "Wait—you did what, now?"

Alex stepped over to a pile of Ellie's stuffed animals' dress-up clothes and pulled out something blue and sparkly. He lifted it up to the moonlight. It was his blue and silver Mexican wrestling mask, the one his uncle Davey had brought him back from Guadalupe. The mask of El Solo Libre, his short-lived superhero identity. He looked down at his N.E.D. suit, then over to the fake mirror that hid the wormhole. He didn't know what was the right thing to do. Glancing back at his El Solo Libre mask, he looked over at the pile of fluffy pals and noticed Herbert's P.U.P.E. helmet. He thought of the person he wished was on the other end. "If only you were here, old buddy. Together we'd split up and take care of that evil old hag *and* exterminate those overgrown weeds."

Beep. The tiniest of sounds broke the silent air as Alex saw the little red light on the side of the helmet suddenly turn to green.

CHAPTER 26

Sammi popped out of the wormhole, tucked herself into a silver ball, and rolled across the cluttered floor of the caveman diorama. She came to a crouch behind a pile of what looked like scrap metal. The MinionBots were scattered in a heap, and Sammi peeked out from behind them, looking for any sign of life—especially Herbert's. It was eerily silent.

"*Herbert!*" Sammi called out. "*Herbert, are you here?*"

"I'm so sorry." A croaky old voice made the hair

stand up on the back of Sammi's neck. "Your friend Herbert's stepped out. You just missed him."

Sammi tried to place the source of the voice. She looked up at the woolly mammoth standing stoically in the corner. It seemed to be coming from him. "*WHAT HAVE YOU DONE WITH HERBERT?*" she cried out. "*TELL ME WHERE HE IS!*"

"*HAHAHAHAHAA!*" The cackling was clearly coming from the mammoth. "*Don't worry,*" the horrible voice continued. "*He'll be back. He has one of my suits, as does your other friend. But they'll both be here shortly to hand them to me.*"

"If you think that, then you're as stupid as you are mean!"

FOOM! A blast sounded from atop the mammoth, and Sammi barely caught a glimpse of a black and gold blur as it flew above her head. It flipped in the air and landed right behind her with a *THUD!*

Sammi spun around—but not quickly enough. *THWACK!* Four mechanical arms shot out of AeroStar's tiara, grabbing Sammi by the wrists and ankles. They lifted her off the ground and held her suspended, directly in front of AeroStar's gaze.

"Hmm . . ." AeroStar walked around Sammi,

examining her from all angles, as if she were window-shopping for a new cape. "Smaller than I remember being, but I can work with this. . . ."

Staring back out at her 111-year-old self, Sammi recognized her own eyes behind the creases, her own hair beneath the gray streaks, her own grin beneath the wrinkles. She took in AeroStar's supervillain costume: the black bodysuit, the large boots, the flowing cape, and the golden Utility Tiara. Sammi couldn't help thinking that she looked strong. Confident. Beautiful, even—but very dangerous.

"I swear, if you harm any of my friends—" Sammi began, but was cut off by AeroStar's horrible laughter again.

"*Please* tell me you're not as dumb as you are puny," the old woman said. "If I wanted you and your friends dead, do you really think any of you would be alive right now? It was never part of my plan to cause the great AlienSlayers *physical* harm. Where's the revenge in that? I only want to take away from them the things they love the most!"

"You don't even know us," Sammi said.

"Please," AeroStar said. "Herbert? Alex? How abut we deprive them of technology and heroism. Good start."

Sammi stared back at her. "How do you think you'll do that?"

"Easy! I'm simply going to trap them in this world, with no way for Herbert to rebuild his beloved G'Dalien technology and no way for Alex to save the G'Daliens or his beloved older self! They'll be stranded here forever, with no way to ever fulfill their dreams!"

"*HA!*" Despite being held helplessly above the floor, Sammi felt good laughing in the face of her evil self. "Then your stupid plan has already failed! You can't trap them *anywhere* so long as they each have a N.E.D. suit—Herbert on this end of the wormhole, Alex on the other! *So there!*"

"My naive little version of me, you haven't been paying attention. I have a secret weapon—the only thing that they both have in common and care about equally." Her mechanical arms pulled Sammi closer, so that they were nearly eye-to-eye. "I have *you*. My dear, you may not have learned yet what I learned long ago—boys are *so very* predictable. Trust me. They'll both be along shortly."

"*Phh!*" Sammi scoffed at her. "Believe me—the *last* thing Herbert or Alex would *ever* do is walk right into your trap."

"*RELEASE HER IMMEDIATELY!*" The voice came from behind them both. It was Herbert's. He was alone. And unarmed. And walking right into the trap.

"Oh, no," Sammi muttered.

"Why, what is *this?*" AeroStar said, pretending to be shocked. "Have you come to make a bargain to save your *friend?* What a complete and utter surprise!"

"That's right," Herbert seethed through gritted teeth. He looked so upset his glasses were fogging up. He held up his N.E.D. suit. "I have what you want, and you have what I want. *Let's make a deal.*"

"*Herbert, no!*" Sammi shouted. "It's a trap! *DON'T GIVE HER THE SUIT!*"

"*Silence!*" AeroStar said, grinning at Sammi. "Don't be so inconsiderate. Your friend here came to save you. At least show some *manners*."

THWACK! In an instant, the mechanical shackles shot back into AeroStar's tiara, releasing Sammi, dropping her to the floor with a *THUD*. Sammi scrambled to her feet—but her stomach dropped as she saw Herbert hand AeroStar his N.E.D. suit.

"Well, that was easy," AeroStar said. "Nice doing business with you." With a *whir!* and a *click!* a small blaster popped out of her tiara and aimed right at Herbert's head. "And now, I think you should run along—as in, *for your life*."

BLAM! The blaster scorched the floor where Herbert was standing. Sammi jumped and knocked him out of the way just in time, and the two of them scrambled away and dived behind the woolly mammoth. *BLAM!* Another blast hit the back wall of the diorama behind them.

"Just so you know"—AeroStar's voice was getting closer—"This blast won't kill you—it'll just put you into a state of shock for a few hours. You'll wake up completely disoriented with a shrieking headache, but rest assured, you'll be *quite alive!"*

"What are you doing?" Sammi said to Herbert as they crouched behind the stuffed creature's tree trunk–like leg.

"Y'know. Saving you?"

"Who asked you to save me? Now she has two of the three N.E.D. suits! One more and she can fulfill her crazy plan!"

"Don't worry." Herbert smiled confidently. *"I have a plan of my own."*

BLAM! Another blast nearly got them, hitting the side of the woolly mammoth. The giant creature teetered back and forth and began falling toward them. Herbert grabbed Sammi's hand and ran along the back wall. *BLAM! BLAM! BLAM!* They were followed by tiara blasts, each just missing their heads.

CRASH! The mammoth fell onto its side, forming a great hairy barrier, trapping them in the corner of the diorama room. A turbo boost blasted from the other side of the fallen beast, and AeroStar flipped in the air, landing perfectly on the overturned mammoth's belly.

"Didn't I tell you?" she said to Sammi, pointing her blaster at the two of them. "Boys are *so* predictable."

BLAM! Another blast hit the wall just above their

heads. In the smoke, Herbert nudged Sammi and gestured for her to look down. She saw they were now standing on some sort of ventilation grate. Beneath the grate under her feet, looking up at her, stood Dallas, Sausalito, and her old friend Chicago Illinois, giving her a thumbs-up. She caught her breath at the sight of them.

"Now, you may want to say good-bye to each other," AeroStar said. "You won't be seeing each other for—well, *forever*."

Sammi and Herbert looked at each other. Herbert winked. Sammi quickly threw her arms around Herbert, hugged him closely and glanced downward. Beneath the grate, the three future boys moved clear. Chicago held in his hand a small device with a button on it.

"*Wow*," Herbert whispered. "You're *good*. Very persuasive performance."

"*No*," Sammi whispered back, still looking down. "*Without me, she'll let you go. This isn't acting. It's really good-bye—but just for now.*" She saw Chicago hold up his fingers and silently count down: *3-2-1* . . .

Ka-chungk! In an instant, the grate swung open, dropping into the floor. Sammi released Herbert and leaped backward in the air, away from him. *BLAM!* A tiara blast hit the back wall just as Herbert dropped through the floor. Rubble from the blast poured down on the would-be rescuers. They peered back up through the smoke. "Sammi!" Chicago called out. "C'mon! *Jump!*"

Sammi picked up a piece of debris from the floor where she was crouching near the fallen mammoth's fanny. She peeked out and saw AeroStar seething atop the stuffed creature's belly, looking around through the smoke for her targets. Sammi hurled the debris at AeroStar as hard as she could.

PTANG! It bounced off her tiara, knocking the golden super weapon off her head "*Aaaaahh!*" AeroStar shrieked, falling backward off the mammoth. Sammi rushed to the open grate.

"Hey, guys!" she said. Chicago grinned, happy to see her smiling face again.

"What are you doing?" Herbert said. "Get down here before she kills you!"

"She's got two suits. I can't let her go through the wormhole, with or without me. I'm staying to fight her."

"Then we'll fight her with you." Chicago grinned, holding his hand up so she could pull him out of the grate.

"No," she said. "I think I can beat her. You guys go. She won't follow you. She doesn't need you. She needs me. I'll be okay. But thanks for trying to rescue me. Now go!"

BLAM! Another blast hit the wall above Sammi's head, raining more debris down into the hole in the floor. Sammi heard her friends scramble away on the other side of a pile of rock and concrete and stood to face AeroStar, who was standing defiantly on top of the mammoth, her tiara back on her head. She was also wearing a much-too-small N.E.D. suit.

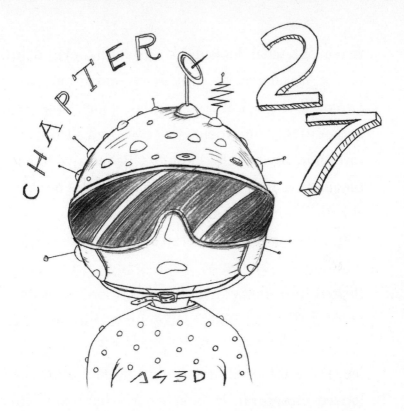

CHAPTER 27

Alex reached out for the Parallel Universe Perspective Enhancer helmet, which was still blinking green. He felt his heart beating like crazy as he slowly lifted it over his head. He lowered it, flipped the visor down, and hit the switch on the console.

It was completely dark, as before. His beating heart sank a bit as his eyes strained to find anything in the nothingness before them. Suddenly, a strange, blurry image began to emerge. Alex squinted to make out what looked like a blobby, cylindrical object. Was it a rocket ship? A weapon of some sort? He couldn't tell, but it was *definitely something*. As it came further into focus, he saw it had a thin, stiff tail on it. *Oh, no,* Alex thought. *He's staring through the glasses at some sort of giant alien rodent!* The object slowly turned in the air. It was floating, but he still couldn't make out any detail on its smooth surface.

Suddenly, a blast of bright orange, goopy string floated into Alex's area of vision. It wrapped itself around the first object, like some alien blanket. *What was this? Some forging of two disgusting alien life forms?* It looked hideous. It looked grotesque. It looked unnatural. It looked—as a hand suddenly reached out for it, revealing its scale—*like lunch.* It was a SuperCheezyFrankOnnaStick—the greatest snack in the entire universe.

Alex watched with anticipation as the hand pulled the goopy cheese-covered weenie closer then lowered it out of his field of vision. A bite's worth of time later, the hand reappeared—with half of the delicious hot dog bitten off.

"He's alive!" Alex shouted, forgetting he was standing in the middle of a dark, two-story dollhouse. "Old Man Alex is alive, *and eating!*" He continued to stare, transfixed by the perspective of his 111-year-old self, somewhere in space, a hundred years in the future. The P.U.P.E. glasses Old Man Alex had swiped must have been an early prototype, because, while Alex could see what Old Man Alex was looking at, Old Man Alex wasn't showing any signs of a reaction at seeing the inside of a *Fluffy Stuff 'n' Pals Teaparty Townhouse.*

"*This is so cool,*" Alex said. "But where in the universe can you be? C'mon, buddy, gimme a clue. . . ." He watched a large sleeve sweep across his view as Old Man Alex obviously wiped cheese off his face. Tears of joy rolled down Alex's cheeks beneath the helmet. Alex caught his breath as suddenly everything he was looking at began to move quickly.

He was looking at the rungs of a long ladder welded to the side of a metal wall, like on the inside of a ship. He watched Old Man Alex's hands reached out in front of his field of vision and grabbed one rung of the ladder after another as he climbed. Finally, they reached an escape hatch, and Alex watched as Old Man Alex's arms opened the hatch then pushed his way up through the hole into what looked to be the bridge, where the captain would steer and control the ship. He spotted control panels, workstations, and monitoring screens, but everything was dimly lit and shadowy. Something struck Alex. "Everything's dark and shut down. The entire ship. So, *why are you wearing sunglasses?*"

Old Man Alex climbed another, shorter ladder above the bridge. This delivered the two of them into an observation tower. It was a fully enclosed glass bubble, and Alex was now staring out at what Old Man Alex was staring out at: the pure, dense nothingness of deep space. Alex couldn't even make out any stars. Mixed with his ongoing excitement was now a slight feeling of dread as he remembered what Old Man Herbert had said about the vastness of space. Even with this incredible invention, how would Alex ever figure out where his 111-year-old self was?

He began to doubt if his 111-year-old self even knew. Maybe this was why Old Man Alex was staring out at the darkness. *But with sunglasses on?*

Then, suddenly, he got his answer. Alex squinted inside the helmet as a sliver of blinding light suddenly sliced through everything else. It was like a sunrise turned sideways. Alex chuckled inside the helmet as he realized why Old Man Alex had the sunglasses on. He could now make out something large and black obscuring the slice of light, and it was much like looking at an eclipse. This is why there were no stars. The blackness he and his older self were just looking out at wasn't space; it was a planet. A dark, black planet.

But now that planet was moving out of the way, to allow something much brighter behind it to peek its way around it. Its light was as strong, as bright as—

"*The sun?*" Alex asked himself. The light began to recede again. It was as if the planet blocking it was moving back in the way—or maybe the floating ship Old Man Alex could no longer captain was drifting back to its initial position. Either way, the light was fleeting again. Alex focused as hard as he could—not on the sliver, but on the round object or planet that was going back to obscuring it. Just before it was engulfed back into darkness, he could make out some details—a ruddy, bumpy, grayish surface, with small mountains, canyons, and craters—then it blocked the light and returned to pure darkness.

When the show was over, a hand reached up and took off the glasses. As they were removed from Old Man Alex's head, the helmet atop Alex's head beeped. The inside of his visor went blank, except for the message that appeared as before:

PARALLEL UNIVERSE MATCHING SUBJECT: OFFLINE.

Alex tore the helmet off and yelled at the top of his lungs, "*YEEAAAAAAH! HE'S ALIVE! OLD MAN ME IS AAALLLIIIIIIVE!*" Looking around for someone to share this incredible information with, he decided the crowd staring at him would have to do. He high-fived four stuffed bunnies, a fluffy llama, eight teddy bears, an orangutan, and a pair of googly-eyed frogs.

He stopped when he spotted his El Solo Libre mask lying on the floor. Standing near the open window, he saw it shimmer in his hands. Alex looked out the window and stared up at the moon. Then he thought about what he had to do next.

CHAPTER 28

BLAM! The blasts were coming faster and closer as Sammi dodged and dived across the floor of the caveman diorama. The only thing keeping her from being blasted was the fact that AeroStar was having trouble moving very quickly in the tight-fitting N.E.D. suit.

"C'mon!" Sammi said as she dived out from behind the heap of MinionBot scraps and rolled across the floor. "You'll have to move faster than that! Maybe you're a bit too big in the behind to be wearing kid's-size clothes!"

"*STAND STILL SO I CAN BLAST YOU!*" AeroStar shouted back, nearly toppling over stiffly in the tiny silver suit. She was careful to keep her back to the diorama railing so that Sammi couldn't escape. "Give up—you and I are going through that wormhole together, so that you can meet your vengeance and I can begin my new reign of total domination!" *BLAMMO!* Another blast missed Sammi as she jumped behind a large heavy piece of machinery.

As AeroStar blasted wildly in her anger, Sammi studied the machine she was hiding behind. "*ClemCorp BoulderMover X-10?*" she whispered to herself. She peeked over it and looked at the cannonlike nozzle mounted on top. She spotted AeroStar creeping through the blast-smoke-filled diorama, and Sammi silently pointed the business end of the nozzle at her. She reached down, found the switch, and, with one last glance to make sure her aim was true, turned the machine on.

FRAAAZZ! The holding beam shot out of the cannon and struck AeroStar. The old woman shrieked as she left her feet and found herself hovering in the air. "*Aaaaaah!*"

Sammi swung the nozzle of the BoulderMover X-10, moving AeroStar over to the middle of the diorama near the fake, painted-on cave entrance. Then she ran out from behind the hulking machine to greet the captive AeroStar. "Wow, did you build that? 'Cause that's really impressive. Seriously, nice work."

"LET ME DOWN RIGHT NOW! THIS IS NOT PART OF MY THREE-AND-A-HALF-POINT PLAN OF VENGEANCE!"

"Yeah, about that . . . I don't see you getting any errands done today, never mind carrying out over-complicated revenge plots." She walked around the helpless old woman, grinning at the sudden reversal of fortune. "To be honest, your little plan wasn't exactly working out even *before* I trapped you with your own invention. I mean, you *still* don't have the third N.E.D. suit. And wasn't there something about stranding Alex here in this world?" She turned to the fake cave entrance and put her ear to it. "'Cause I don't think I hear him—"

WUBBA-WUBBA-POP! Sammi jumped back from the fake, painted-on cave wall as it suddenly melted into a bright blue, shimmering wormhole entrance.

The next second, Alex came flying out of it, fists first, superhero style.

"AAAAAAH!" He was in his full El Solo Libre outfit—Mexican wrestling mask, beach towel cape, silver N.E.D. suit with his tighty-whities on the outside. He sailed out of the wormhole, straight into the ball of energy holding AeroStar and knocked the old woman out of the beam, replacing her with . . . himself. AeroStar went skidding across the floor as Alex found himself hovering in midair. He looked around at the scene—the

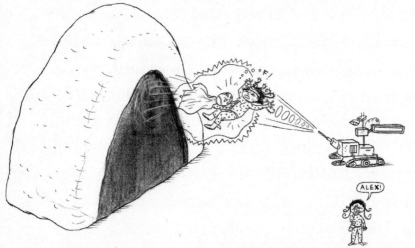

trashed diorama, the toppled mammoth, Sammi standing in shock, AeroStar struggling to stand up—and delivered his best attempt at a superhero entrance. "Uh . . . El Solo Libre is here?"

Over the cruel cackling of AeroStar, Sammi dropped her head in defeat. "Oh, Alex," she said. "This really isn't helping."

"*Oh, but it is!*" AeroStar said. She was on her feet now, her tiara blaster trained on the two of them. "El Solo Libre, *my hero!* I don't know *what* I would've done if you hadn't arrived just in time!" The old villain laughed as she hit a small button on the back of her tiara. The mechanical claws extended from her headgear, reaching into the ball of energy. They quickly spun Alex around and stripped him. They pulled the third empty N.E.D. suit out of the energy ball—leaving Alex floating in nothing but his tighty-whities and the Mexican wrestling mask his uncle Davey had brought back for him from Guadalupe.

WELL THIS IS EMBARRASSING.

"*Alex!* I told you to stay and protect the present!" Sammi was careful not to make any sudden moves. AeroStar's blaster was aimed right for her head.

"I had to come!" Alex said, trying to cover up his underwear as he floated helplessly above the two females staring up at him. "I found something out! Old Man Me is alive! He's floating helplessly in space, but he's alive!"

"That's wonderful news," Sammi said. "But—"

"Yes!" AeroStar stepped forward. "Have fun knowing he's alive while having no possible way to ever find or rescue him for the rest of your life—*El Loser Libre!*"

She tucked the extra N.E.D. suit under her arm and grabbed Sammi. "As for you, I think it's time you and I fulfilled the final point-and-a-half of my three-and-a-half-point plan. Ooh, which reminds me."

She picked up her clear clipboard and pressed a button on the top. Her checklist was projected above them. She touched the glass, checking off the third and third-and-a-half boxes. "There. It so helps to be organized about these things."

"*What are you going to do with me?*" Sammi shrieked.

"Sammi!" Alex shouted. "*NO! LET HER GO!*" He wiggled and squirmed inside his floating ball of light but couldn't break free.

"You two are so cute," AeroStar said mockingly. "It may help to know that in a few moments, Sammi won't be the same person you knew and loved. The journey she's about to take with me is going to be quite—*transformative. HAHAHAHA!*"

"*NOOOOO!*" Alex screamed as AeroStar flipped the switch on Sammi's N.E.D. suit then on her own. The wormhole pulsed to life, pulling at the two activated suits. AeroStar turned her head and her tiara blasted a fiery red beam at the ClemCorp BoulderMover X-10. *KA-BLAM!* It exploded in a ball of fire and thick, black smoke.

The beam cut out, and Alex dropped to the floor, covering his face from the sooty air all around him. He scrambled to his feet and lunged toward the wormhole.

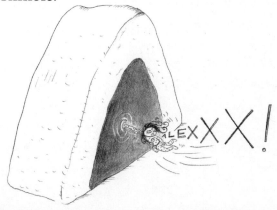

"ALEX!"

Sammi and Alex reached out their hands, but the wormhole engulfed AeroStar and her hostage. Alex cried out as he watched them disappear into the wormhole and then the wormhole transform back into a solid wall. *FOOOMPH!*

"SAMMI!"

An eerie silence fell over the diorama. Just the smoking husks of the ClemCorp machines could be heard hissing behind Alex as he pressed his hand against the fake, painted-on cave entrance, wanting more than anything in the galaxy to feel Sammi's hand reach back out and grab it.

POP-POP! The swirling blue wormhole inside the fake sticker decal mirror on the upstairs wall of the *Fluffy Stuff 'n' Pals Teaparty Townhouse* burped out a pair of large silver wads as the two Sammis hit the floor in a crumpled heap. They stirred then slowly stood up, as if from a long sleep.

Sammi rubbed her head. She looked disoriented as she glanced around the plastic room filled with stuffed animals. "What . . . is this place?" she asked weakly. "Have we arrived? *Have I done it?*"

AeroStar sat up with some trouble and glanced

around as well. "Whoa," she said. *"I feel funky."*

"WAIT A MINUTE!" Sammi leaped up, got into a fighting pose and glared at AeroStar. *"YES! I CAN SEE MYSELF WHEN I LOOK AT YOU! AND—AAAAAAH!"* She looked down at herself, shocked by what she saw. *"YES! I'M A CHILD AGAIN! IT WORKED! THE WORMHOLE HAS SWITCHED US! THE FINAL, HALF-POINT PART OF MY PLAN HAS COME TO FRUITION!"*

AeroStar—or the person who *looked* like AeroStar—stumbled to her feet and looked at the fake decal mirror on the wall. *"No! How could this happen?"* She was grabbing her wrinkly face, staring at her new reflection in disbelief.

"You see, *dearie*," the real AeroStar (who looked like Sammi) said, "that old fool Herbert left files on his supercomputer that were *filled* with interesting information about wormhole travel and the effect of parallel universe people crossing paths. I was particularly interested in theories pertaining to what might happen if two parallel people were to *travel through the wormhole together.*"

"No," Sammi was saying, running her bony fingers through her gray-streaked hair. *"Please, please, no . . ."*

"Oh, stop whining," AeroStar said. "This isn't even your punishment. Well, not entirely. I've simply deprived you of what you love the most." Sammi was so shocked she didn't even struggle as AeroStar unzipped her N.E.D. suit for her and pulled it off her 111-year-old body. "I've sentenced you to live out the short remainder of your old age in a world without Herbert or Alex, just as I've done." AeroStar plucked the tiara from the top of Sammi's gray-streaked hair and put it on her own. Far too large, it slipped down over her nose. She pushed it back up and joined Sammi in staring at her wrinkled face in the mirror. "And I'm afraid, *at your age*, you're far too old to make any new friends." She mock pouted at Sammi's horrified expression. "That is your punishment—and my revenge."

Sammi turned to her. AeroStar stood grinning. Her tiara wobbled on her head as it produced a small blaster, which after she readjusted the headgear again, aimed directly at Sammi. It was strange for Sammi to be threatened by her own body, knowing what kind of person was inside of it, controlling it, *being it*. She tried to process all this, and then thought of something.

"Of course," Sammi said. "*That's* why you are what you are. You never got to know Alex or Herbert like I did. Instead of having friends, you worked hard, practiced hard, did everything *hard*. But you didn't have any fun. Without fun, it just became about winning. At everything. No matter what, no matter how. And when you got outdone by G'Daliens, or outsmarted by three kids from the past, all you could do was get back at them. You're strong, you're powerful, you're mean, but the one thing you can never be—*is me*. And more important, because I had the best friends in the world, because I knew Alex and Herbert, I'll never be like you. No matter what I look like on the outside."

AeroStar stared at Sammi for a moment, which is to say she stared at her very own, very old, former face. She saw the deep lines of scowling from years of anger. She felt a tingle of sadness rise deep in her belly, but she shut her eyes and shook it off, causing her tiara to fall around her ears. She pushed it back up.

"Oh, grow up," she shot back. Realizing she'd accidentally made a joke, she burst out in a fit of nervous-sounding laughter. AeroStar looked around out of habit, to yell at the MinionBots for not joining in, then abruptly stopped as she remembered the two of them were alone. "So. You've got me all figured out. Well, even if *anything* you said were true, it wouldn't matter. I have a new body, a new start, and I'm off to begin a new life."

She slipped off her own N.E.D. suit and laid it in a pile with the other two. "I figured if I'm going to the trouble to destroy the lives of you three, why not reboot my own life while I'm at it? Swapping bodies with you made me a young girl again, and now I'll use that to get people to trust me. I've got all the time in the world to slowly build my empire, until I finally rule this idiotic planet. When those G'Daliens show up, this time I'll be ready for them, the people will stand with me—and we'll destroy them, *together.*"

"You won't get away with it," Sammi said.

"Granny, *please*. I already have! I may look young, cute, and innocent, but I have a century's head start in knowledge and experience! I've been to the farthest corners of the galaxy, outwitted an entire race of advanced aliens, built machines capable of destroying their advanced technology—I've even beaten and bested the world-famous AlienSlayers! Tell me, what *on your earth* is going to stop me from taking over this boring, little twenty-first-century town in, say, three-and-a-half seconds?"

"*EEEEEEEEEEEAAAAAAAAAAAAHHHHHHHH!*"

The entire teahouse shook as an Audreenian Non-Carnivorous Giant Podling Plant, sounding dangerously close, made its horrible noise.

AeroStar froze. "*What—was that?*"

Sammi grinned. "Oh, didn't I mention? We've had a little alien problem here in the present. Seems on the last mission you sent him on, your best employee took it upon himself to do some *freelancing*."

AeroStar began to tremble. She glanced around the tiny dollhouse. She clenched her entire body. Then she lost it, and screamed. In Sammi's voice, of course. *"GOOOOOORRRRRR-DONNNNN!"*

The G'Dalien came bounding from the house out onto the deck. *"SAMMI! IS THAT YOU? HOLD ON! I'M COMING!"* He face-planted in the backyard and squirmed himself back up onto his tentacles. He squeezed through the door to the tea party town house and somehow slither-stumbled up the narrow stairs. When he got to the top, he froze at the sight of AeroStar (who was actually Sammi). Shocked, he looked for answers in the face of Sammi (who was actually AeroStar). He was a *very* confused G'Dalien. And they hadn't even started talking yet.

CHAPTER 31

Herbert could barely see a thing as he led Chicago, Dallas, and Sausalito down the long, dark underground tunnel, but he could smell where he was going. Sizzling pepperoni, sausage, and linguica wafted all around him and grew stronger with each step toward Andretti's Pizzeria. By the time they reached their home base, Herbert's mouth was watering like crazy. Mr. Illinois had been busy.

So had Old Man Herbert. "Bad news," he said, fiddling with his makeshift homing map. "I've been tracking the MagnaWreckers. They all seem to be smashing things they've already destroyed. Most troubling."

"Why would they be doing that?" Herbert asked.

"I would hypothesize that they've stopped receiving programming orders. This would cause them to default back to their first directive and recrush earlier targets. My theory is that AeroStar stopped transmitting orders because she's gone through the wormhole—with no intention of returning."

"*The Flee-a-seum!*" Dallas gasped.

"What about it?" asked Herbert.

"That arena was the centerpiece of the G'Daliens' city," Old Man Herbert said. "So it was the first thing AeroStar had the MagnaWreckers destroy. The humans moved in after the machines moved on, thinking they'd be safe. But now—"

"They're coming back," Herbert said. "And this time, it'll be full of people."

"They won't know what hit them," Sausalito said.

"We have some time," Old Man Herbert said, peering at the foggy screen of his device. "Without direct orders, the Wreckers are moving slowly, stopping to resmash whatever they come across along the way. But once they converge on the main road that leads straight into the Flee-a-seum, there'll be nothing to stop them."

"Except us!" Dallas said.

"Yeah, but how? I mean, what do we do?" Sausalito said.

A voice called out from behind them.

Everyone spun around to see Alex, standing just inside the pizzeria. "We build a spaceship and we fly to the dark side of the moon."

"Alex? What are you doing here?" Herbert said.

"Me? Oh, nothing. I just single-handedly fixed your P.U.P.E. helmet, figured out where Old Man Alex and the G'Daliens are stranded, then came back here to save them. That's all."

"*Ahem.*" Old Man Herbert objected to at least one part of that account.

"Oh, really?" Herbert said, picking up on his

elder's signal. "Then you can tell me where I went wrong. Was it the hypothalamus input receptors? No! I had the neural transmitters crossed, didn't I?"

"Er," Alex muttered. His brain booster had long since worn off, and he was now having trouble remembering what he'd had for breakfast. "The point is I fixed it. And now I'm here to lead us on our heroic rescue mission."

"Uh-huh," Herbert scoffed. "Well, you're too late, because I've got the situation under control. After all, I single-handedly led everyone to AeroStar, rescued Sammi from *certain death*, and am now devising a plan to save the humans before the MagnaWreckers crush them. You're welcome to help, of course. Just try not to get in the way."

"*Ahem.*" Old Man Herbert gave Alex a signal this time.

"Oh, *really?*" Alex pretended to search behind the door, inside a pizza box, under his shoe. "So where *is* Sammi? Because I'm pretty sure I just saw her get taken into the wormhole with AeroStar. So *there!*"

Everyone stared at Alex. The smirk slowly faded from his face. "What?"

"*You're* the one who let AeroStar escape?" Dallas asked.

"And with *Sammi*?" Herbert added.

Alex glanced around the room nervously. "Uh . . . it wasn't my fault! Who puts an evil villainess in a holding beam *right in front* of a wormhole portal? Total rookie move! I came to save *you*, by the way. How did I know I'd pop outta the wormhole, knock AeroStar free while trapping myself, allowing her to take Sammi back to the present along with all the N.E.D. suits, leaving us stuck here without a way home?"

The room got very quiet. Herbert buried his face in his hands, then took a deep breath and looked up at Alex. "So that's it, then. We've got no way home, no weapons, no technology, and we've gotta save a floating ship full of G'Daliens on the dark side of the moon as well as an arena full of humans on the other side of town. Did I leave anything out?"

Everyone looked over to Alex. "Just one thing," he said as a slow grin began to stretch across his face. "We're gonna do all that for Sammi."

The others gathered around the rooftop of Andretti's Pizzeria as Old Man Herbert yanked the camouflaged tarp off the SkyLimo. He circled the vehicle in his hovering airchair, tapping it with a metal device, checking it out. "Okay," he said. "I can make this airtight and space-worthy. The challenge will be getting it to achieve escape velocity."

"Translation?" Alex said.

"He means we need to figure out how to launch it," Chicago said, "so it can escape the earth's gravitational pull."

"We have to get this clunker from zero to eleven point two kilometers per second," Herbert said. "*Without* G'Dalien technology."

"How are we gonna get that kind of blast?" Alex said.

"'S'cuse me, guys." Mr. Illinois poked his head out of the rooftop stairwell. "I got seven hundred fifty pizzas ready for delivery. If you think that's enough, I'll let the brick oven fire burn out. It's already nearly a thousand degrees." He chuckled. "You could launch a *rocket* off that thing right now."

The giant pilotless MagnaWrecker mindlessly wailed away stupidly on what was left of a large

TransPorter tram that had long since crashed to the ground. Alex and Dallas snuck up on it and jumped on the tailgate of the wrecker. They held on tightly as the machine jerked violently with each slam of the magnetic wrecking ball. Alex climbed to the exhaust pipe, which burped black, sooty smoke out the top of the wrecker, and signaled that he was ready. Dallas pulled out of a large backpack an enormous white, tube-shaped object, about the size of a fat wiener dog. Marked on the side were the words *ANDRETTI'S QUALITY MOZZARELLA CHEESE*. He handed it up to Alex, who lifted it above his head and, timing between bursts of belching black exhaust, dropped the cheese tube into the pipe. It fit like a torpedo in a firing chute.

The MagnaWrecker stopped suddenly. A strange, creaking groan echoed from deep within it. Alex and Dallas leaped from the back of the wrecker and rolled behind a slab of moving sidewalk that was upended nearby. The great destroyer began to rattle. Black soot began to seep out of the seams of the machine as it shook more violently by the second.

KA-BLOOOOOOM! The side panels blew off the

MagnaWrecker, leaving a skeletal frame of its insides fully exposed. As its crane swung around wildly, Alex and Dallas charged through the belching black soot now pouring from the wrecker. They beelined for the ClemCorp FuelRod—an inky black log about the size of a scuba tank attached to the machine, and the power source of its engine. The two boys tugged at it as the MagnaWrecker bucked and swayed.

CHUNGK! The FuelRod snapped out of its casing, sending Alex and Dallas falling backward with it in their arms. The MagnaWrecker shuddered, seized up, and collapsed in a hunk of steaming scrap. Alex and Dallas high-fived each other, then quickly stuffed the black battery into their bag and lugged it back to Andretti's.

The tall, four-story brick restaurant had been converted into a hidden launchpad. A large circle had been cut in the roof directly over the large round, brick pizza oven below. The mayor's old SkyLimo was crudely suspended by sacks of flour so that it stood vertically with its nose pointing skyward at the hole, its tail just a few feet above the empty brick oven. Strapped to its back end were dozens of ClemCorp FuelRods. Chicago and Herbert entered behind and dumped their haul into the oven.

"Stopped another one right in its tracks!" Herbert exclaimed. Alex smiled at the fun Herbert was clearly having taking down the clunky destroyers.

"Good work, boys," Old Man Herbert said. "By my calculations, the thermodynamic temperature should be sufficient for successful escape velocity."

"Is the cabin secure enough for space travel?" Chicago asked.

Mr. Illinois held up a glue gun. "My top secret cheese combination mixed with high-grade silicon adhesive. Sealed every nook and cranny."

"All right, then," Alex said. "Let's light this candle!"

Old Man Herbert and Mr. Illinois watched with pride as the young space travelers climbed a ladder and boarded the oddest rocket ever assembled. The 111-year-old Herbert monitored his old-school computer terminal while Mr. Illinois pulled the flame-resistant camouflage tarp tightly around the bottom of the ship, sealing it to the top of the pizza oven.

Herbert, Alex, Chicago, Dallas, and Sausalito settled into the cockpit, shut the bubble glass behind them, and strapped in. As Mr. Illinois sealed the hatch from the outside with his homemade, top secret, high-grade, super-strong mozzarella-silicon combo adhesive, Old Man Herbert's voice crackled from the dashboard. "Okay, you ready, boys?"

"Ready as we'll ever be," Herbert said nervously. He had a history of "launching" his lunch in this very vehicle, and that had been without dozens of industrial-strength, super-concentrated rocket fuel logs strapped to its fanny.

"Okay, then," Old Man Herbert shouted back. "Five . . . four . . . thr—"

"*ORDER UP!*" Mr. Illinois suddenly shouted. He lit the fuse inside the brick oven, slammed the steel door shut, and tackled Old Man Herbert to the floor.

KA-BLOOOOOOOOIIIIEEEEEE! The logs burst into a black-sooted blaze of power and shot the SkyLimo out of the roof like a bottle rocket. The flames and soot blasted the entire downstairs of Andretti's, singeing the few hairs Old Man Herbet had on his head and completely covering him and Mr. Illinois in black dust.

"We have liftoff!" Old Man Herbert said, coughing up the thick air.

They both stared at the sky for a moment. "We sure do!" Mr. Illinois said. He looked happier than he had in a long time. "You hungry? I was thinking I might whip up a couple of calzones."

CHAPTER 32

AeroStar was yelling at a slightly confused GOR-DON. "I ordered you to do a simple task: get the AlienSlayers to come back through the wormhole to me. *All three of them.* Not only did you fail utterly at that task, you managed somehow to release aliens into this world! *DO YOU KNOW HOW THIS UPSETS MY THREE-AND-A-HALF-POINT PLAN, YOU OVERSIZED SPACE GUPPY?*"

GOR-DON stared, then broke into a grin. "*HA-HA!* Excellent imitation of AeroStar, *Sammi!* That sounded exactly like how she yells at me when she's mad!"

"I'M AEROSTAR! SHE'S SAMMI, YOU IDIOT!" AeroStar shouted back up at him. *"WE SWAPPED BODIES WHEN WE CAME THROUGH THE WORMHOLE TOGETHER!"*

GOR-DON stared down at her then looked over at Sammi.

"It's true," Sammi said sadly. "Is Alex's family okay? Where's Ellie?"

The confused G'Dalien blinked for a second, trying to piece all of this together. "Uh, Ellie's over with Herbert's mom," he finally said. "The Filbys went into town to head off the pod-plants."

"That's good, I guess," Sammi said, looking down at her new body. "Although, I don't know how I'm going to explain this to *my* mom."

GOR-DON looked from her to AeroStar then back to Sammi again. He plopped down in one of the tiny tea party chairs. "*Oy.* I need a nap."

"What you need," AeroStar said, "is a kick in your slimy, worthless butt! Why did you introduce aliens to this world? *What were you thinking?*"

"I already told you last night—"

"I thought if I introduced a few Audreenian Non-Carnivorous Giant Podling Plants into the ecosystem and let them scare the humans for a bit, I could come along and tame them or something. Then maybe she'd see me as, I dunno—"

"A *hero*," AeroStar said. A slow grin spread across her face. "That's *genius!* I can't believe I didn't think of it myself! That would save me *years* of slowly earning the trust of these apes! All I have to do is let the— What did you say you planted?"

"Audreenian Non-Carnivorous Giant Podling Plants."

"Highly effective." AeroStar grinned. "But no match for my tiara blaster." She tapped it proudly, causing it to slip down over her nose again. She adjusted it. "I'll let the podling plants run amok for a bit, wreak some havoc, destroy a few neighborhoods. Then I'll swoop in, defeat them, save the city, and become a hero to the moronic citizens of Merwinsville! I'll be a legend by lunchtime!"

"Pretending to save the city to become a fake AlienSlayer," Sammi said. "What a novel plan. I wonder how you *ever* thought of it."

"Yes, the irony is sweet," AeroStar said. "You and your phony friends may have done the fake alien slaying thing *first*, but just you watch—I'll do it *best*." She turned to GOR-DON, who was now beginning to look more depressed than confused. "As for you," she said. "I've decided to spare your life, seeing as you *accidentally* improved my already perfect Three-and-a-Half-Point Plan of Vengeance. I guess I'm in the mood to grant *second chances* today." AeroStar tossed the three N.E.D. suits at the glum G'Dalien. "Destroy these. Burn them. Do you think you can handle that?"

"*What?*" Sammi's head snapped to GOR-DON

then back to AeroStar. "You *can't*! What about my friends? What about *me*? *I'll be stuck in this body forever!*"

AeroStar looked back at her. "*Ech*. Is that really how my voice sounds?"

Sammi glared at GOR-DON, trying to sense what he might do. Her fate, as well as the fates of Alex and Herbert, was literally in his hands. Her heart sank when she heard his mumbled answer.

"I'll see that they're destroyed, my queen."

"GOR-DON, *no!*" Sammi yelled, trying to get through to him. "You don't have to do what she says anymore! You were miserable under her rule, *remember*? You could send those through the wormhole for Alex and Herbert to find right now and end her plan, once and for all!"

AeroStar adjusted her wobbly tiara blaster at Sammi. "Oh, will you *please* stop nagging him in that *dreadful old voice*! He wouldn't dare fail me twice! Besides, he's smart. He wants to be powerful so he can maybe attract another lunch lady! He'll stay on the winning team: *MINE!*"

She prodded Sammi toward the stairs. "Now move. I know just the place to lure the plant aliens—

and I'm going to make sure you have a front row seat."

Sammi walked out ahead of AeroStar, whose tiara blaster was pointed at her head. She looked back at the dejected G'Dalien. He didn't look back. He was slumped over, holding the N.E.D. suits, staring down at his tentacles.

As the ClemRod-fueled SkyLimo rocketed up, up, and out of the earth's atmosphere, Herbert, Alex, Chicago, Dallas, and Sausalito felt like their faces were being yanked backward by an invisible force. When they finally leveled off, the opposite feeling kicked in: they were in zero gravity, and it was as if the powerful, invisible grip on them had suddenly let go completely.

Alex grinned at Herbert. "How awesome was *that?*" Herbert swallowed hard, trying to keep his stomach from doing triple somersaults.

After a while, Old Man Herbert's voice crackled from the dashboard. "You should be coming up on the moon now. We're going to lose communication with each other as you go around to the dark side, which means you'll have to take over manual control of the ship."

"Yes!" Chicago said, pumping his fist. He'd been miffed ever since he found out that navigation would be controlled from the ground and he wouldn't be able to drive. Chicago loved to drive.

Alex looked out at the blinding white side of the moon and saw LunaPark. What had once been a beautiful public play space filled with humans and G'Daliens looking for some low-gravity fun was now empty and abandoned. As the dark side of the moon approached in the window like a black curtain, Old Man Herbert's voice crackled one last time.

"Okay, you're coming up on it now. I'll speak to you on the other side, hopefully with some good news. Good luck, fellas. We're all counting on y—"

Fzzt. The radio crackled and went silent. A shroud of shadow fell across the SkyLimo as it floated around the dark side of the moon. The boys sat in silence, peering out at the pitch-black curvature of the moon's dark side, searching for any sign of a giant transporter ship.

"It should be out here somewhere," Alex said. "It's *gotta* be."

The SkyLimo got very quiet and still. With every passing second a feeling of dread grew in their stomachs. *What if they weren't here? What if they never found their G'Dalien friends again? What if—*

WUMP! The SkyLimo bumped into something— hard. "What was that?" Dallas said.

A crack in the cheeze-glue holding one of the seams suddenly gave way. "Everyone, oxygen helmets, NOW!" Herbert yelled.

They scrambled with helmets and suits as Chicago steadied the ship and jerked the wheel. "Hang on," he said. "I got this! We're under control! I just—"

WUMP!

This bump knocked the side panel of the SkyLimo and sent them into a slow spin. Herbert felt his stomach lurch.

"Sorry! Sorry!" Chicago yelled out. "I'm steadying the ship now, but—" *WUMP!* "Okay. We might have to bail in a minute, guys. FYI."

"Look! There!" Sausalito suddenly yelled.

They pushed their helmets against the glass as Chicago steadied the SkyLimo. There in front of them, camouflaged against the starry sky, was a black mass of something very, very large floating in space. As they got closer, Chicago suddenly got a good idea. He hit a button on the dashboard marked *HEADLIGHTS*.

The light cut through the darkness and bounced off the dark hull of a massive ship. Centered in the beam of light were the words *S.S. Clemtanic*. They stared at it in disbelief. Alex beamed.

"We found them!"

Then the headlights blinked out as their SkyLimo lost power. "Uh, guys," Chicago said. "I think it's time to abandon limo."

Alex was the first to exit the dead husk of their homemade rocket. He pushed himself off it and floated over to the S.S. *Clemtanic*, grabbing its side like a flea clinging to the side of a great dane. Herbert followed, then the others. They all slowly, weightlessly crab-crawled up the side of the hull to the top of the ship. There they found panels and radar dishes, pipes and sealed hatches that they could grab and use to pull themselves along as they searched for a way in. But the farther they inched along on the top of the black, lifeless ship, the worse they began to feel about what they might find inside.

Alex came to a large hatch with a steering wheel–size release lock on it. They all tugged at it, trying to get it to budge. "Let me try," the beefy Dallas said. Pulling at it with all his might, he suddenly slipped and nearly went sailing into deep space. Sausalito reached up, grabbed his friend, and pulled him back down to the ship.

Alex desperately knocked on the hatch. "Hello! Anybody home?" Herbert watched, trying not to think about what it would mean for him and his friends if they ended up stranded on an empty, floating ship with no way to get or contact home. He began to calculate how much air they had in their oxygen helmets and started to panic. "Stop!" he snapped at Alex. "You're wasting your time and quite possibly your air!"

Alex ignored him, banging away like a bongo drummer on the door. Herbert couldn't take it any longer. He pulled Alex away from the hatch and, with his back to it, began yelling at Alex. "Listen, you fool. We're on an enormous vessel in the silence of space! There's nothing you can do to get the attention of anyone inside that—"

CLANG!

Something slammed into Herbert's fanny, sending him spinning off the hull of the ship, whirling head over feet, deeper into space.

Herbert grew dizzier and dizzier. He felt like he was going to pass out. Just before he did, two hands grabbed his feet. Through blurred vision, Herbert saw what had to be a hallucination. Old Man Alex's face, as big as the moon, wearing odd futuristic sunglasses, beamed right in front of him. The last thing Herbert thought he saw was Old Man Alex's hand holding up a goopy cheese-covered hot dog on a stick. Then everything went black.

Herbert opened his eyes and blinked. Although it was dark, he could make out the faces of Chicago, Dallas, and Sausalito leaning over him, smiling down. "Did you guys die, too?" he asked. Before they could answer, Herbert's eyes noticed leaning in behind them dozens of G'Daliens. They were all grinning at him. "Am I—are we all—*in heaven?*"

Suddenly, popping into his field of vision in front of everyone was Alex, with a big grin on his face. "Not yet, ol' buddy!" he yelled. "And look who else is here!"

Like an older, goofier evil twin, Old Man Alex's face popped up. He and Alex had their arms around each other and were laughing like the best of friends.

"Hiya, Herbie!" Old Man Alex said. "Sorry about bumping you off the hull! Glad you're feeling better, and just in time, too—we're about to crank up the welcome party!" He slipped on the futuristic P.U.P.E. sunglasses he'd swiped from Old Man Herbert and yelled down to someone. *"OKAY, BOYS! MOVE THOSE TENTACLES!"*

With a loud *WHIR*, a blinding light suddenly washed over him, followed by the loud cheering of a large crowd all around him. Thumping party music blasted, and Herbert sat up. As he did, the cheering multiplied. He looked around to find himself strapped across the waist to a table perched high on a pedestal in the middle of a massive ballroom filled with G'Daliens. They were dancing and flipping and flying through the zero-gravity room, and they were very happy to see him. Herbert adjusted his eyeglasses and peered over the edge of his perch. Far below him, on the floor, were rows of stationary exercise bikes hooked up to a large generator in the corner of the room. Pedaling on the bikes were some of the fittest G'Daliens Herbert had ever seen. They waved up at him without breaking stride.

"Ingenious!" He laughed as he looked up to see Dallas and Sausalito spinning around in the disco lights provided by the pedal power below. They were ecstatic to be bouncing around in zero gravity with their little G'Dalien pal EL-ROY.

Herbert looked to the other side of him and saw Chicago somersaulting high above the ballroom floor. "We did it, Herbie!" he yelled. "We found 'em!"

Herbert laughed again as he unbuckled his belt and pushed off the table he'd been resting on. He'd barely begun soaring into the air when a dozen G'Daliens flew up alongside him and hugged him and belly-bounced him over to a new group. He was so happy to see them all, he almost forgot about the mission they were on. Only when he was finally caught by a familiar face did it all come crashing back.

"Welcome to the party ship, Herbie!" Alex said. He was now wearing his elder self's P.U.P.E. glasses and was munching on a SuperCheezyFrankOnnaStick. "Isn't this *great*? I told you I figured it out! I saw him in the ol' P.U.P.E. helmet, and here we are!"

Here we are. This struck Herbert and sobered him up. It all rushed back to him: their mission, the humans, everything that was at stake. He looked at Alex and angrily ripped the glasses off his head. "*STOP, ALL OF YOU!*" he yelled. "*We don't have time for this! Earth needs our help! THIS PARTY IS OVER!*"

Everyone stopped and drifted until they bumped

into a wall, the ceiling, or each other. The pedaling G'Daliens stopped, too. The lights dimmed; the music slowed to a stop. Floating there in the dark, Herbert heard Alex's voice.

"Leave it to Slewg to travel all the way around the dark side of the moon, just to P.U.P.E. on the party."

CHAPTER 34

In their new, swapped-out bodies, AeroStar now stood a little more than half Sammi's size as she forced her along the sidewalk toward the center of town. Helping her effort, AeroStar had her head-mounted tiara blaster aimed squarely at the small of Sammi's back—although since AeroStar's head was a bit smaller, the tiara kept slipping down.

Sammi had never felt so low. She kept wondering if GOR-DON had already destroyed the N.E.D. suits. She wondered how she'd be able to live without her friends, and in this wretched body she'd been trapped in.

"Where are you taking me?" Sammi asked. "You got your twisted revenge on us. Why don't you just let me go? I need to make sure my family's okay."

"Keep quiet and keep moving," AeroStar snapped back. "I'm not done with you. I want you to bear witness as I gain the love and adoration of your mindless friends and neighbors and even your family."

Sammi hadn't thought about this. What if this evil shrew, in *her* body, were able to trick her *own family*? Her mom was always pushing Sammi to be the best at everything—seeing her daughter save the city might be enough to make her overlook the fact that this new Sammi acted *nothing* like the real Sammi. She had to break free. She had to find a way to somehow make things right again.

"*EEEEEEEEEEEAAAAAAAAAAAAHHHHHHHH!*"

The shrieks of the Audreenian Non-Carnivorous Giant Podling Plants were coming more often. She just hoped they hadn't done too much damage, hurt anyone, or worse.

SCREEEECH! Suddenly, a flurry of dust and skidding bicycle tires surrounded the two of them. AeroStar looked around in a panic as Moose, Adriana, and the rest of their crew jumped off their bikes and fell to their knees in front of her.

"Thank goodness, I found you!" Moose said. He seemed to be near tears.

"Please, please, *protect me*!" Adriana added, nudging Moose aside.

As the others made their case for who she should save first, AeroStar beamed down at them. "Now this is more like it." She grinned. "Your begging pleases me. On your feet!"

Sammi's classmates scrambled to their feet, pushing and shoving as they jockeyed for position.

Moose spoke first. "Sammi, er—*AlienSlayer Sammi*, I mean—we know you have the power to defeat these weed monsters! One of them tore up the football field at our school! You have to stop them—*you're our only hope!*"

"Sammi, your majesty, or whatever, listen to *me*," Adriana pleaded. "The ballet studio near my house? One of those horrible creatures stepped on it and crushed it! That's where you and I *first became best friends!*"

Sammi rolled her eyes. "Give me a break. We

were never friends. You used to put gummy worms in my ballet slippers—"

"*SILENCE!*" AeroStar had stepped out from behind Sammi, but her tiara blaster was still trained on her. "Do not criticize my *biggest fans!*"

Moose, Adriana, and the others grinned at this, happy that they were winning over the girl they thought was their savior. "Tell us, great and mighty slayer," Moose said eagerly. "What can we do to help you save our city?"

AeroStar smiled at Sammi, who was looking more and more angry by the second. "*This is gonna be even easier than I thought,*" she said out of the side of her mouth to her hostage. "I'll tell you all what to do," she exclaimed loudly to the hopeful crew. "I need you to disperse and spread the word. Tell everyone to come out of their hiding places and head downtown. To the pizzeria! For it is there that I will lure, fight, and finally *defeat* these vile creatures who dare lift a petal against our fair city of *Merwinsville!*"

The bike bullies let out a cheer. They pushed Sammi aside and lifted AeroStar on their shoulders. Moving quickly, Sammi bunched her cape up and leaped onto Adriana's bike. Without looking back, she began pedaling as fast as she could back toward her neighborhood.

"*Three cheers for Sammi! Hip! Hip! HOORAY!*" The kids bounced AeroStar above their heads and began carrying her toward the center of town. AeroStar glanced back to see Sammi pedaling up the hill. She shrugged and yelled after her over her newfound admirers. "Go, old woman! You're of no further use to me. For now I have people who like me! *Who really like me!*"

As Chicago, Dallas, and Sausalito reunited with their little G'Dalien pal EL-ROY, Herbert explained to Old Man Alex how he and his passengers had been tricked by AeroStar, breaking the bad news that she never had any intention of allowing them to reach the G'Daliens' home planet. Alex stood nearby, happily munching on SuperCheezyFrankOnnaStick.

"Well, I guess that makes me a first-class *space-schmuck*," Old Man Alex said. "I just figured after a while she'd send us up some reserve fuel, and we'd be back on our way. While we waited, the G'Daliens took apart the ship's exercise room and rigged these temporary generators. That gave us enough energy to run the essentials: SuperCheezyFrankOnnaStick machine, music system, and, of course, disco lights. Every night as the sun peeked out from behind the moon, I'd go up to the captain's deck to look for any sign of a supply ship. Then I'd go back down and we'd crank up the party. I was *so* wrong about these G'Dalien dudes, by the way. Not only are they not evil—they're crazy-good dancers!"

"They also happen to be geniuses," Herbert said.

"*No duh!* Have you ever played tic-tac-toe with them?" Old Man Alex asked. "They win, like, *every single time!*"

Alex giggled at this. Herbert rolled his eyes.

"So how long would you have waited until you figured out you'd been tricked and abandoned by AeroStar?" Alex asked.

"Gosh, I don't know. I'm a pretty easygoing dude. Besides, she helped me once before, when the G'Daliens first came to Earth. I was young and scared and very vocal in my hatred for them. When everyone turned against me, AeroStar was nice enough to offer me a place to hide out for a while."

"*She stuck you in a cave for fifty years,*" Herbert said. "So you'd be blamed when she got rid of them!"

"Right, right. I always forget about that part." Old Man Alex scratched his head. "Maybe I'm *too* easygoing."

"Don't feel bad," Alex said. "She tricked everyone. And I hate to tell you this, but after she exiled you and the G'Daliens, she destroyed everything they created. The city's a wasteland. The humans are in hiding, and they're in very serious danger. Time's running out, and we need all hands—or tentacles— on deck to save them."

"I'll get my best pedalers goin'," he said. "We'll turn this tub around!"

"I'm afraid that won't work," Herbert said. "I've run diagnostics on your manual power system. The G'Dalien generators may satisfy your party needs, but they won't provide nearly enough energy to get us back to Earth."

Old Man Alex thought about this for a moment. "Hey, you guys remember that crazy Death Slug dude?"

Herbert looked at him. "If you mean the 'dude' I was served as a snack to before he chased us all over the surface of the moon and then flew to Earth to devour us, then yeah, rings a bell."

"What if he gave us a tow?" Old Man Alex said. "He's super strong, and I'm not just talking about his odor."

"I don't understand," Alex said. "Where would you find him?"

"Mr. Nibbles? He lives across the way. Pops in to party with us from time to time," he answered, slipping on his sleek future-shades. "Last time he had a few too many snacks and puked all over the place. Took us days to clean up. So he kinda owes me a favor."

Old Man Alex led Herbert and Alex into the bridge. Alex recognized this place as the room he'd seen through the P.U.P.E. helmet. When his older self led them past the darkened control panel and up a shorter ladder, Alex grinned. He knew *just* where they were headed.

The observation tower was situated in the topmost part of the ship and was essentially a 360-degree glass bubble. Staring out from here, Alex and Herbert felt like they were floating free in space, without an enormous ship beneath them.

"Now," Old Man Alex said, picking up a square of shiny metal. "Let's see if I can get this to work. It's a little tricky." He slipped on his P.U.P.E. glasses and readied the reflective square, staring out into space. "Oh," he said. "You two may wanna squint. You don't want to get your eyeballs all *scorchy*."

Alex and Herbert looked up just in time to be blasted by a sliver of light as the sun peeked out from behind the dark side of the moon. They averted their eyes to Old Man Alex, who was holding the metal up to the incredibly bright sunlight. "We broke this reflector panel off the roof of the ship when we were first stranded. Works pretty well, but you have to catch the angle . . . *just right. . . .* " He maneuvered the metal square around until the sunlight suddenly hit it, reflecting back out into space, shooting a

solid square beam of light straight down at the dark side of the moon.

As he moved the square around, Old Man Alex softly sounded out a message. Herbert thought he heard him mutter the words "emergency," "help," and "Mr. Nibbles."

A minute or so later, the sun crept back behind the dark side of the moon, just as Alex had seen through the P.U.P.E. glasses in his sister's dollhouse.

"There," Old Man Alex said. "My handwriting's not great, but they'll get it. They always do."

Plunged back into darkness, Alex's and Herbert's eyes readjusted so they were able to look out at the dark side of the moon. Written across part of its surface in fiery orange was:

S.O.S.
Need help!
Bring Mr. Nibbles
—Cap'n Alex

Herbert's mouth hung open.

Alex was grinning, his eyes as wide as lunar craters. *"That's awesome, Cap'n Alex!"*

"Wha—how—why does that work?" Herbert said.

"Little trick I picked up living down there all those years," Old Man Alex said. "MoonBat guano— *their poop*—it's phosphorescent! And there's this one valley where they do their business. Totally full of it, you might say. Kinda like a giant litter box. Nasty, stinky place, *horrible for camping.* Anyway, since it's phosphorescent, it absorbs light! Stays lit-up for an hour or so. Kinda fun to play with—makes for a good little message board, too."

"It's like a giant poop-filled Etch A Sketch!" Alex said. *"I wanna try!"*

"Sure!" Old Man Alex beamed. "But you'll have to wait till tomorrow. Sun peeks around there for just a minute a day. You can have your turn, and Herbie, you can go the day after that. Sound fun?"

"No," Herbert said soberly. "Sorry to be the party pooper again, but if we're still here in two days, all the people down in that Flee-a-seum will be gone, forever."

Herbert's words hung in the air, until Old Man

Alex broke the silence.

"You're a real bummer, you know that?"

All the G'Daliens on the entire S.S. *Clemtanic* were dancing and floating excitedly in the G'Dalien cyclist–fueled ballroom, getting ready to welcome a very special and very large outside guest to the party. As a massive pressurized chamber slowly began to open, cheers went up throughout the room, matched by a mighty bloodcurdling "RRRRREEEOOOOAAAARRRR!" A second later, the chamber door burst open, and into the ballroom flew the vilest creature in all the galaxy: a ferociously terrifying Klapthorian Death Slug. Specifically, it was Mr. Nibbles, the Klapthorian Death Slug Herbert had had the displeasure of being roommates with.

"*Oh, no,*" Herbert said, cowering behind Alex and Old Man Alex. They were grinning ear-to-ear as they watched the great slug-beast wildly circle the ballroom. Suddenly, to Herbert's horror, Mr. Nibbles stopped and sniffed the air. He jerked his multieyed head and looked *directly at him.*

"*RRRRREEEOOOOAAAARRRR!*" The Death Slug

charged. Herbert froze, shutting his eyes and fully expecting to be gobbled up. The beast opened its razor-tooth-filled mouth and descended on Herbert. At the last second, it stopped short, stuck out its sofa-sized tongue, and—*sluuurrrp*—licked his face.

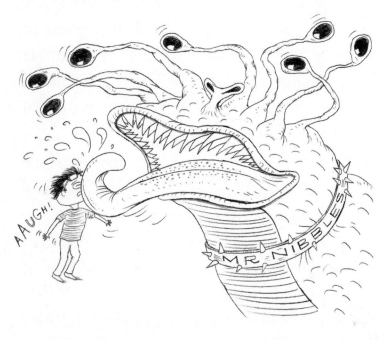

"*Uggggh!*" Herbert opened one drool-covered eye to see Mr. Nibbles panting and smiling at him like a giant playful golden retriever. He gave a quick, barklike roar and licked Herbert's face again, his nubby slug tail wagging happily.

"*Nibbly! You stop that this instant!*" a voice called

out as Herbert wiped the thick, syruplike slug drool from his face. He saw a heavyset woman he recognized as Marion, the former lunch lady and AlienSlayer Fan Club president, slide off the back of the giant creature.

Marion must have added "Death Slug Trainer" to her resume, because as soon as she put a fat finger in his face, Mr. Nibbles sat obediently. She spoke to him sternly. "That is no way to greet a guest, you silly ol' slug!" She patted him on the nose and tossed him his favorite snack: a large freeze-dried MoonBat.

While Mr. Nibbles munched away on that, Marion ran straight up to Alex and gave him a massive hug. "Wow! AlienSlayer Alex, live and in the flesh! Long time, no see!"

Alex beamed at the sight of his biggest fan, then chuckled at Herbert, whose hair was slicked back with slug saliva. "Hiya, Marion. We could really use your help if it's no trouble."

"Help an AlienSlayer? It'd be an honor, wouldn't it, Nibbly?" Marion and her pet grinned.

Herbert finished wiping the slug drool off his glasses and put them back on his head. "We're gonna need . . . um, Nibbly to give us a tow. It's crucial we're pulled low enough to the moon's surface so we get caught in its gravitational pull. By the time we circle the light side of the moon, we should have all the momentum we need to boomerang around it and steer straight for Earth."

"No problemo!" Marion said.

"I'm no scientist, but if we get caught in the moon's gravity, won't we crash into it?" Old Man Alex said.

"Yes. If we don't have enough approach speed, we'll hit the moon like a brick. I've calculated the data, and with a ship this size, it's essential that we reach a speed of *at least* thirty-nine point three meters per second."

"Well, *Nibbly?*" Alex asked the oddly quiet Death Slug. "Whaddya got in ya?"

As if trying to answer, Mr. Nibbles sluggishly raised his head. Everyone turned to him—he didn't look quite right. He opened his mouth slowly and—BLEEEUUUUUURRRRCCCHHH!—threw up all over the ballroom floor, coughing up the SkyLimo.

Awesome!" Alex exclaimed, turning to Herbert. "Did you *see* that?"

Herbert, now splattered with Death Slug vomit,

was busy remembering fondly the saliva that had covered him just moments ago.

Marion was quick to apologize to Old Man Alex. "I'm so sorry, captain! I know this happened last time, too! It's just, there's so much space junk floating around out there—he's always gobbling up stuff that he shouldn't! *Bad Nibbly!*"

"I still say that was the gnarliest thing I've ever seen," Alex said. "C'mon, Slewg. Even you've got to admit that was awesome."

Herbert held his nose and stepped up to inspect the semi-digested SkyLimo they'd abandoned. Checking the area where they'd lost their side panel, he turned to EL-ROY. "There's still some unburned fuel in here that didn't ignite at liftoff. Can you and your crew get this thing to run?"

"I got this," EL-ROY said seriously. "C'mon, guys!" Chicago, Dallas, and Sausalito stared at the chunky, puke-covered ship for a moment, then held their noses as they stepped up to help slide it across the slug puke–covered ballroom floor.

*T*he M.U.L.C.H. group was hanging off a large daisy-sticker-covered pickup truck in the middle of the main intersection in the center of town. In the driver's seat, leaning on the horn, was Mrs. Filby. In the back of the truck, surrounded by the other M.U.L.C.H. members, was a giant container with a spray hose on top. The container was marked *ECO-FRIENDLY, NONTOXIC, FULLY ORGANIC HERBICIDE*—FATAL IF SWALLOWED.

The reason the truck wasn't moving and the horn was honking was because it was nose-to-nose with *another* truck in the middle of the same intersection. This one was a camouflaged, military-looking vehicle armed with telescopes, satellite dishes, and multiple antennae. On the side of the truck were the letters M.E.G.A.—and all of that group's members, including Mr. Filby, were hanging off the back of it, yelling at the yellow truck blocking its way. In the flatbed part of the truck was a huge stainless steel tank with a hose on the top. It was marked *LIQUID NITROGEN-BASED CRYOGENIC GAS SPRAY*—APPLY WELCOMINGLY!

The two honking trucks filled with yelling M.U.L.C.H. and M.E.G.A. members were clearly in disagreement on how best to take care of the invaders.

"These are evil weeds capable of anything! They must be choked and killed—*organically!*" yelled Mrs. Filby to the M.E.G.A. truck.

"Are you *crazy?!*" Mr. Filby hollered back. "These specimens are more scared of us than we are of them! We must freeze them temporarily so that we can study them and find out how best to make them feel welcome and accepted by our planet!"

RRRRUUUUUMMMMBLLLE! The two truckloads

of protesters stopped to listen for a moment. The thudding root-steps of the pod-creatures were getting closer, and from different directions. They listened for another moment, then launched back into their intersection argument.

"Green-thumbs!"

"Freak-seekers!"

The standoff continued, growing so heated that not one adult from either side noticed an evil supervillain from another time and parallel universe and disguised in the body of an eleven-year-old girl being carried on the shoulders of a group of local schoolkids.

In front of Andretti's Pizzeria, AeroStar jumped off the shoulders of her newfound fans and turned to them. "Thank you, *my new minions!* Now—I command you to go forth and tell the entire town to come to this spot, where they will witness the birth of their new savior—*ME!*" Moose, Adriana, and the rest of the kids cheered loudly, then ran off in all directions to do their new master's bidding.

Inside Andretti's, AeroStar threw open the doors to the abandoned restaurant, closed her eyes, and took a deep whiff. The brick oven had been left burning, and there were a few overcooked meat-lovers pizzas cooking inside. "Ahh, the sweet, meaty smell of vengeance," she said. She ran into the walk-in refrigerator and pulled out giant slabs of Canadian bacon as well as a few more pounds of sausage, then threw them into the pizza oven. As the meat sizzled in the fiery pit, she ran up the stairs to the roof.

AeroStar exited the stairwell, walked to the ledge, and looked out at the city below. Now and again she would hear the distant roars of the Audreenian Non-Carnivorous Giant Podling Plants coming from four different directions. AeroStar pulled the grate off the exhaust vent jutting out of the roof. She could smell the sizzling meats wafting out of the oven below and pointed the vent up into the breeze.

"Come and get it." She grinned.

GOR-DON stood over a makeshift bonfire he'd created out of the mangled barbecue parts Mr. Filby smashed with a wrecking ball. Feeling the heat of the fire, the sad G'Dalien looked down at the three N.E.D. suits in his arms and thought about what he was about do. He knew that once he dropped the suits into the hungry flames below, he'd seal AeroStar's rule, secure the horrible fates of the AlienSlayers, and never see Marion again. On the other tentacle, he couldn't escape the thought that if Marion somehow knew what he was about to do, she'd never want to see him again anyway.

He *really* needed that nap.

Staring off through tear-filled, glassy black eyes, GOR-DON looked over and happened to spot the garbage bin beside Herbert's house. He held the suits out over the fire—and took a deep breath.

CHAPTER 37

LO-PEZ was one of the largest, roundest, blobbiest G'Daliens Herbert and Alex had ever met, which was saying something. But he was an excellent driver, especially in an emergency. He'd navigated Herbert, Alex, and Sammi through many sticky adventures in the past—and this time was no different.

The roly-poly G'Dalien was overjoyed to see his two old friends, and even more thrilled to do whatever he could to help save the humans back on Earth, especially his old partner, Mr. Illinois. The fact that he got to help by driving the SkyLimo was like frosting on a box of cupcakes. He barely stopped giggling as he flew Chicago, Dallas, Sausalito, and EL-ROY to the front of the S.S. *Clemtanic* so they could attach the two ships with makeshift towing cables.

"*Yeeeeeeee-Hawwwwww!*" Marion's holler came out of the built-in walkie-talkie speakers and bounced inside everyone's bubblelike oxygen helmets. She, Alex, and Herbert sat on the back of Mr. Nibbles, who was hovering just in front of the S.S. *Clemtanic*. There was a long towline connecting his giant nubby tail to the nose of the enormous ship. Standing in the captain's bridge, looking out at them through the window, was Old Man Alex, ready to give the signal.

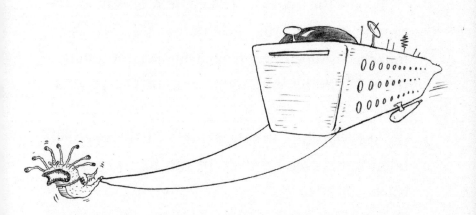

"Okay," Old Man Alex yelled. *"ONE, TWO, THREE—HEAVE!"*

Herbert snapped the reins, and Mr. Nibbles let out a *RRRROOOOAAAAARR* as he began flapping his wings and moving his tail. LO-PEZ slammed his chubby tentacle down on the gas pedal, and the SkyLimo lurched into overdrive, tugging away at the ship.

"HEAVE! HEAVE! HEAVE!"

The S.S. *Clemtanic* creaked and groaned as it began to move very slowly. It crept forward behind the writhing slug and the grinding G'Daliens. The ship began to creep steadily, gaining momentum and a little speed as it headed toward the white horizon of the bright side of the moon.

Inside the cockpit, Old Man Alex sat in the captain's chair, a big grin across his face as he munched a SuperCheezyFrankOnnaStick and steered the S.S. *Clemtanic* straight for that bright white horizon.

"It's working! It's working!" Herbert yelled, holding his free hand up in the air like a rodeo cowboy.

"This is SO COOL!" Alex added. He, Herbert, and

Marion all tossed their heads back as Mr. Nibbles pulled harder ahead of his cargo.

"YEEEEE-HAAAWW!"

The ship began to drift faster and faster as the gravitational pull of the moon took hold of it. Old Man Alex kept it as close to the surface as he could without slamming into the mountaintops on the moon, all the while watching the speed pick up. "Little faster, boys . . . *little faster!*"

Attached to the nose of the colossal ship, Mr. Nibbles and the SkyLimo bore down and strained to go faster. As they rounded the bright side of the moon, the S.S. *Clemtanic* began to overtake them.

"Okay, boys!" shouted Old Man Alex. "That's it! You did it! Cut 'em loose!"

Chicago, Dallas, Sausalito, and EL-ROY ran to the back of the SkyLimo and detached the towlines as LO-PEZ veered off to the right and away from the ship.

Alex slid down the back of Mr. Nibbles and cut the line attached to his enormous tail. Looking up, he saw the S.S. *Clemtanic* about to crush them. "*Pull up! PULL UP!*"

Herbert and Marion yanked back on the reins, and

Mr. Nibbles let out a *REEEOOOOOOAAAAAARRRRR* as he zoomed straight up, out of the line of the *S.S. Clemtanic*, now cruising at a steady clip toward Earth.

Alex plopped back behind Herbert and Marion, and the three of them watched the ship cruising below them. "We did it!" Alex yelled. "They're heading home!"

Herbert studied the ship as it passed below. "They're gonna come in too fast," he said. *"We have to do something."*

"What?" Marion asked, glancing back at Alex. "What did he say?"

"He's a glass-is-half-empty guy," Alex said. "You

kinda get used to it."

Herbert ignored them both. "Captain Alex. Can you slow the ship down?"

"No, but why would I wanna?" Old Man Alex's voice crackled back in his ear. "We just got this tub *movin'*!"

"At this rate, I'd approximate you have three hours until impact."

"Dude, did you say *impact?*" Old Man Alex said.

"I hadn't foreseen this variable. Strap all G'Daliens in for a bumpy landing. We'll zoom down ahead of you and see what we can do." Herbert kicked Mr. Nibbles with his heels and let out a roaring "*Hee-ya! Giddyup!*" The slug burst ahead of the ship.

Alex leaned past Marion and stared into the bubble helmet at Herbert's face. "*Giddyup?*"

Outside Andretti's, Old Man Herbert spotted something high in the sky. It was a tiny dot, but it was growing bigger by the second. "That can't be—" he muttered. He checked the mini-monitor on his airchair armrest. "There's something coming in, and it appears to be *completely organic* in compositional makeup. But what living organism could be that large?" He stopped, looked up at the dot, which was now coming in fast and sluggy. "Oh, *no.*"

Old Man Herbert wheeled his airchair around and bumped into Mr. Illinois, knocking him onto his lap. He then zoomed behind the parked delivery tank. They peered up as the object crash-landed right in front of them.

BLUBB-BOING! The giant Klapthorian Death Slug's belly hit the parking area in front of Andretti's, then bounced a good hundred feet forward and up into the air. The beast did a double somersault and flopped back down, skidding sideways into the side of Andretti's, making a nice Death Slug–sized dent in the brick wall. Then it was still.

Old Man Herbert and Mr. Illinois cautiously came out from behind the building.

"*Yeee-Hawww!*" a voice called out. Marion popped up, her hair mussed and crazy-looking inside her cracked space helmet. She was beaming like a cowgirl at the rodeo. "I gotta say, since I started working with this beast up on my MoonRanch, that was some of the best slug wranglin' I've ever seen!"

Old Man Herbert and Mr. Illinois looked to the top of Mr. Nibbles's head to see who she was talking about.

Herbert stood up uneasily. Alex joined him and waved in a daze as Herbert smiled oddly. "Thanks. Amazingly, that's actually the first time I ever did that." He fell forward off his slimy steed, face-planting in front of Old Man Herbert. Mr. Nibbles lovingly licked the back of his head.

Old Man Herbert and Mr. Illinois took the three travelers inside and fed them some pizza. They were thrilled to hear that the S.S. *Clemtanic* had been found, and everyone was healthy, happy, and headed back to Earth.

"But unfortunately, at a lethal rate of speed," Herbert quickly added, souring the celebration yet again. "Given that and their angle of approach, they'll crash-land right down Main Street in precisely two hours forty-seven minutes, give or take. Ideas?"

"That might give us enough time to evacuate the Flee-a-seum," Alex said. "Or else those people will be squashed by the S.S. *Clemtanic* when it skids down Main Street."

"No. We couldn't get there safely," Old Man Herbert said. "The MagnaWreckers are on the move. It's too dangerous. We took a lot of them out when we stole their FuelRods, but a good fifty or so are heading straight for Main Street. Once they merge onto it, it's a direct line to destroying that shelter and everyone inside of it."

Herbert thought for a moment then looked over at the Andretti delivery tank. "Hey, Mr. Illinois," he said. "That homemade, top secret, high-grade, super-strong mozzarella-silicon combo adhesive you used to seal up the SkyLimo for space travel—you got any of it left?"

"Couple of vats," he said. "You know me, once I get going in the kitchen . . ."

Alex smiled at Herbert. "You're thinking of

slowing 'em down, aren't you?"

"Who?" Marion said. "The S.S. *Clemtanic* or the MagnaWreckers?"

"Both," Alex and Herbert said at the same time.

Sammi sped up to Alex's house on Adriana's bicycle, rode around to the backyard, and jumped off, letting the bike slam into a hedge. She ran into the *Fluffy Stuff 'n' Pals Teaparty Townhouse* and tore through it, looking everywhere for the G'Dalien who held the key to undoing all this mess. GOR-DON wasn't anywhere inside, nor were the N.E.D. suits. She ran back out into the yard and stopped short. Her heart sank as she saw the barbecue pit, still smoldering, the ashes a grayish black. She dropped to her knees and cried.

"No! It can't be! How could he do this?" Thinking about Alex and Herbert trapped in that desolate future world, Sammi buried her face in her hands. She felt the saggy skin around her cheeks and eyes. She pulled her hands away and stared at her bony, wrinkled fingers. *And I'm stuck in this body until I die,* she thought. It was over.

"*EEEEEEEEEEEAAAAAAAAAAAAAHHHHHHHH!*"

The pod-plants were close, and getting closer. Sammi knew AeroStar was somehow luring them downtown, where she'd have her moment of glory. Sammi wiped her baggy eyes, stood up, and took a deep breath. "If I'm stuck in this old body, I may as well use it—*to kick my own butt.*"

AeroStar had amassed a pile of meat-based fuel on the rooftop of Andretti's Pizzeria. Slabs of ham and bacon, logs of sausage and pepperoni were all stacked beside the open pizza oven vent, which spewed its meaty smells skyward. She picked up a greasy tube of linguica and dropped it down the vent. She heard a *THUD* and a *sizzzzzle.* The wafting aroma immediately blasted out even stronger. She tossed a few more chunks of succulent meat into the vent and walked casually over to the edge of the rooftop. Below she could see the M.U.L.C.H. and M.E.G.A. trucks still in a standoff and, beyond them, coming down nearly every street, the crowds of townspeople looking around carefully for signs of the invaders, curious as to who or what would save them.

"That's it, my future minions, step right up. Come witness your new hero save your pathetic town so you can make me your queen!"

Sammi ran as fast as her elderly legs would carry her toward the center of town. She was soon blocked by slower-moving crowds of her fellow Merwinsvillians, none of whom recognized her or even batted an eye at her bizarre super-villainess getup. Everyone was looking to the treetops, trying to make their way to Andretti's without being stomped on by an overgrown, uprooted weed beast.

"Hey!" a familiar voice called out to her. "Hey, old lady! Stop!" Sammi turned to see Moose pedal up to her, with Adriana sitting on his handlebars. "You're that weird old bag who stole my bike!" Adriana said, pointing at Sammi.

"Didn't your mother ever teach you respect for your elders?" Sammi said.

"*Whatever*," Adriana snapped back. "We don't have to listen to *any* grown-ups now, especially one dressed up in baggy yoga pants."

"That's right," Moose chimed in. "AlienSlayer Sammi put *us* in charge of getting people down to the pizzeria to witness her *greatness*."

"Well, we'd better get down there, then," Sammi said.

"Not so fast, *gramsy-pants*," Adriana spat, hopping off Moose's handlebars and stepping up to her. "I want my bike back. Now WHERE IS IT?"

Sammi glanced over their shoulders at something behind them. "Oh," she said. "I left it in a hedge, just up the street—the Filbys' house, second to last on the left. Feel free to go and get it. Of course, you'll have to get past *him*."

"*EEEEEEEEEEEAAAAAAAAAAAAHHHHHHHH!*"

Just a few houses away, an Audreenian Non-Carnivorous Giant Podling Plant crashed through Mr. Doherty's garage, picked up his garbage bin, and stomped its clawlike root-feet directly toward Sammi, Moose, and Adriana.

"*Aaaaaaaggggh!*" With nowhere to run, the two middleschoolers held each other tightly, frozen in terror. Sammi pushed Moose and Adriana out of the way as the plant beast raised the metal bin over its head. Just before it was about to slam it down on Sammi's head, it stopped. *Sniff! Sniff-sniff!* It puffed up as its olfactory cells in its stalk and leaves inhaled deeply. Sammi smelled it, too: there was a delicious odor of linguica in the air. The podling plant tossed the garbage bin over its shoulder onto Mr. Doherty's

front lawn. Then it stomped away from the three of them, in the direction of the meaty smell, straight for the center of town.

"You're welcome." Sammi jumped on Moose's bike and rode off in the same direction. Adriana and Moose, still hugging, released each other and ran after her.

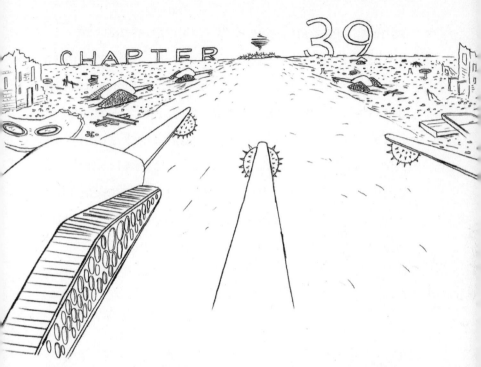

CHAPTER 39

The MagnaWreckers rumbled their way onto Main Street and began barreling toward the last large G'Dalien structure they could mindlessly smash: the Flee-a-seum. Even though the great arena had already been demolished, its walls were so high that they had merely toppled in on themselves, forming an enormous lean-to, tentlike structure. It was the perfect shelter for the humans hiding out in a wrecked and abandoned city, but it was about to become a deathtrap as the Wreckers approached, programmed to slam their heavy, magnetized steel spheres against the already unstable structure.

Andretti's Official Pizza Delivery Tank rumbled out of the pizzeria and onto Main Street Merwinsville, quickly catching up to the parade of destructors. Inside, Mr. Illinois looked through the periscope as Alex took aim. Old Man Herbert followed from above in his airchair, keeping an eye on the approaching wreckers. "You've got one at three o'clock," he said. "Ready . . . aim . . . *goopitize!*"

The tank's cannon raised, took aim at the MagnaWrecker, and—*SPLORT!*—shot out a spurge of Mr. Illinois's homemade, top secret, high-grade, super-strong mozzarella-silicon combo adhesive. It covered the MagnaWrecker's tank treads, stopping it in its tracks right in the center of Main Street. A few other wrecking-ball machines slammed into it with a *CRASH!* Alex quickly turned the cannon on those, too. *SPLORT! SPLORT! SPLORT!* After a few quick blasts, they were quickly stuck to the road.

"Yeah, Herbert!" Alex said. "Your Goopy-Cheeze Battle-Blaster is a success!"

They raced ahead, gooping each and every MagnaWrecker they came upon, leaving Main Street behind them littered with stuck wreckers, their treads gummed up and glued to the road, their strong magnetic planks and spheres still humming. After a hundred or more successful *SPLORTs*, they finally reached the Flee-a-seum ruins, where a few MagnaWreckers were bashing away at the already unstable walls.

Inside, the humans hiding out beneath the giant rubble gathered together in the center, helplessly listening to the horrible crashes and smashes getting closer and closer. The walls trembled and shook with each slam from just outside while the citizens of Merwinsville huddled together and hoped for a miracle.

SPLORT! SPLORT-SPLORT! A strange sound

outside the walls was heard, and then the bashing and crashing stopped. They didn't know what was going on out there, but they knew that the Flee-a-seum ruins around and above them stopped shaking and cracking.

Outside, the Pizza Delivery Tank stopped and turned around. Alex, Herbert, and Mr. Illinois opened the hatch as Old Man Herbert zoomed up to them excitedly. "Nice shooting, Alex," Mr. Illinois said. "You got 'em all!" Looking back, they saw the entire road dotted with hundreds of MagnaWreckers completely gunked up and glued in place. The magnets were humming and the steel wrecking balls were suspended in air from the magnetic force, but they were helplessly stuck in place.

"I gotta hand it to ya, Slewg," Alex said, smiling at the MagnaWrecker speed bumps. "I like this invention of yours a lot more than the day it splorted me in the face with goopy-cheeze."

"I tried to tell you it just needed a little calibrating," Herbert said. "But it wouldn't have worked without the proper ammunition." He turned to Mr. Illinois. "I had no idea you were such an exceptional chemist. That adhesive compound you came up with is quite impressive."

"Better than MightyGlue!" Alex said.

"Tastes pretty good in a spinach calzone, too." Mr. Illinois smiled back.

A small beep emitted from Old Man Herbert's airchair. He looked at the readout. "Gentlemen, now we'll see if the second step of your brilliant plan works as well as the first."

A massively large shadow overtook them, and they looked up to see what it was: in the distance, on the other end of Main Street, the S.S. *Clemtanic* was coming in for a very fast landing. The goop crew abandoned their tank and ran behind the massive door of the Flee-a-seum, taking cover and warning the humans inside to do the same. There was an unbearable moment of silence, then an incredibly loud noise as the colossal cruise ship slammed into downtown Merwinsville with a

The S.S. *Clemtanic* hit the far end of Main Street and slid straight toward the Flee-a-seum, obliterating the road as it carved a valley-sized path through the center of town, leaving in its wake a wide trench with walls of dirt and debris.

GUNGK! GUNGK-GUNGK! Smaller metallic sounds could be heard as the ship plowed through town. The glued MagnaWreckers' magnetized planks and wrecking spheres attached themselves to the *Clemtanic's* metal hull as it passed by.

GUNGK! GUNGK-GUNGK! Each wrecker was torn between its magnetic cling to the ship and its homemade, top secret, high-grade, super-strong mozzarella-silicon combo adhesive cling to the road below. The road lost the tug-of-war every time, but after a few dozen of the heavy machines attached like tiny anchors to the bottom of the vessel's hull, it began to have the hoped-for effect: it was slowing down the destructive behemoth. And just in time, too, as the S.S. *Clemtanic* was running out of road and fast approaching the end of the line: the broken-down Flee-a-seum filled with humans.

GUNGK! GUNGK-GUNGK! A few dozen more MagnaWreckers latched onto the S.S. *Clemtanic*. The enormous cruiser groaned and creaked as its nose slowly ... softly ... *just barely* ... touched the wall of the Flee-a-seum—and came to a stop.

The air stood perfectly still for a moment as the dust settled in the wake of this massive disturbance. Then, a horrible sound—

CREEAAAAAAK ... The barely-touched wall of the Flee-a-seum began to lean inward ever so slightly. The crumbling, creaking sound grew louder and more horrible as the wall began to fall, threatening to topple over on a large group of people standing just inside. The humans saw it coming down and scampered to run clear of it, but it whooshed down like a giant flyswatter, so fast that many had no chance of escaping.

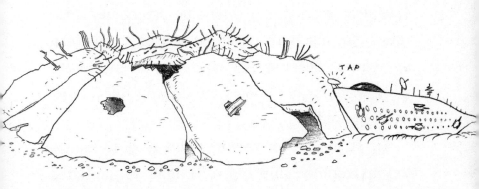

ROOOAAAAARRRRRRR! Suddenly, the wall stopped in midair, just a few dozen feet from the ground, at an impossible angle. The people looked up. Mr. Nibbles hovered overhead with Marion on his back. The wall was held in a lasso, with Mr. Nibbles holding it back with his mighty jaws. Alex, Herbert, and Mr. Illinois quickly herded the humans away from the wall. Once they were clear, the Death Slug dropped the wall. It hit the ground with a dusty *WHUMP!*

With the entrance wall to the stadium now lying on the ground like a massive welcome mat, the humans walked over it and stepped outside for the first time in a long, long while. They looked up at the great ship marooned in the middle of the street, as well as the deep gash it had left in its wake trailing for miles behind it. A large door on the S.S. *Clemtanic* opened. An inflatable emergency slide rolled out. The humans stared at it hopefully then burst into cheers as Old Man Alex emerged with a big wave for his hometown crowd. *"Ahoy, there, dudes and dudettes!"*

He stepped aside to allow masses of G'Daliens to leap from the ship and slide down to the elated crowd below. Cheers and laughter and tears of joy met them, and a happy reunion kicked off with a bang.

Mr. Illinois made his way through the welcoming party, followed by Old Man Herbert in his airchair. The ex-cop/bodyguard/pizza-maker/cheese chemist frantically searched the happy G'Dalien faces for one chubby face in particular.

"Look out below!"

Mr. Illinois looked up and beamed as LO-PEZ, in all his gluttonous glory, came flying down the escape slide, his arms and more than a few tentacles filled with SuperCheezyFranksOnnaStick. *POW!* He plowed into Mr. Illinois, sending the two of them tumbling across the ground in a slippery mess of goopy cheeze. Even with the mess, Mr. Illinois came up smiling. He looked at his old partner and laughed, and LO-PEZ dropped his snack (something he'd never done before) and gave Mr. Illinois a rib-cracking G'Dalien-style bear hug.

Alex, Herbert, Old Man Alex, and Old Man Herbert peeled off from the festivities and ran back up to the Museum of Human History. They stood inside

the trashed caveman diorama, saddened as they realized that Sammi was really gone.

Nothing to be said, the four of them sadly headed back down the Hallway of Human History to rejoin the reunion. As they reached the end of the long hall, Old Man Alex stopped and turned to look back.

"What's wrong?" Alex said.

"Did you hear that?" Old Man Alex said. "It was like a faint . . . *pop, pop, pop. . . .* "

CHAPTER 40

The four Audreenian Non-Carnivorous Giant Podling Plants followed the smell of roasting meat into the center of Merwinsville, converging as they headed straight toward the bickering M.U.L.C.H. and M.E.G.A. trucks. The arguing groups didn't notice they had company—*giant, clod-stomping, meat-craving, alien-plant* company—until the horrible creatures were directly above them.

"*EEEEEEEEEEEAAAAAAAAAAAAAHHHHHHHHH!*"

The members of the two trucks scrambled into attack positions, racing to pump their primers, turn on their valves, and aim their spray hoses.

"FREEZE—*if you please!*" Mr. Filby yelled up from his liquid-nitrogen sprayer at the plant monster closest to him.

"DIE—*organically!*" Mrs. Filby yelled up from her organic herbicide duster at her intended target.

The husband and wife shared a competitive glance, narrowing their eyes as if they were about to fight each other. Then they yelled at the same time: "*FIRE!*"

Both sprayers—one filled with organic herbicide, the other with liquid-nitrogen spray—blasted upward. Mrs. Filby hit the Audreenian Non-Carnivorous Giant Podling Plant standing on the far right. Mr. Filby hit the Audreenian Non-Carnivorous Giant Podling Plant on the far left. Both trucks cheered wildly.

"*EEEEEEEEEEEAAAAAAAAAAAAAHHHHHHHH!*"

The plant monster struck with the herbicide began to swoon and sway, coughing and gasping in the yellowish gas.

Its leaves and roots slumped and wilted, and it began to fall. The plant monster struck with the liquid-nitrogen gas stiffened as the silvery white powder immediately froze it where it stood. Icicles formed off its leaves and roots, and it stiffly began to topple.

BOOM! SMASH! The poisoned Audreenian Non-Carnivorous Giant Podling Plant crashed down on top of the M.E.G.A. truck, completely destroying the tank of liquid nitrogen, sending the M.E.G.A. members diving for cover. The frozen Audreenian Non-Carnivorous Giant Podling Plant fell the other way, landing square on top of the M.U.L.C.H. pickup truck, destroying what was left of the herbicide tank, and sending the organic gardening enthusiasts scrambling. Both plants were only slowed down momentarily, however, and shook off their foreign substances—and now they were *really* mad.

"EEEEEEEEEEAAAAAAAAAAAAHHHHHHHH!"
The other two Audreenian Non-Carnivorous Giant Podling Plants let out a squeal for their fellow monsters and began stomping madly at the scrambling M.U.L.C.H. and M.E.G.A. members, who were running in circles like bugs trying to avoid being squashed. Mrs. Filby tripped and looked up as a massive root-foot came crashing down toward her.

CRUNCH! Mr. Filby grabbed his wife and dived with her out of the way just in time. She smiled at him as he carried her to safety. *"My Mega-man,"* she said.

The townspeople who'd gathered to watch the spectacle they were promised suddenly rallied to help their M.U.L.C.H.- and M.E.G.A.-membered neighbors. They picked up whatever they could find—bricks, rocks, trash cans, chunks from the demolished trucks—and began to attack all four of the pod-monsters.

"NOOOOO!" A scream was heard from the nearby rooftop of Andretti's Pizzeria. AeroStar was standing on the edge, looking down. "You can't save *yourselves!* This is my moment of glory, you simpleminded *morons!"*

"Ahem—" a voice croaked from the stairwell behind AeroStar. "That's my town you're talking about, *sister*."

AeroStar spun around. Sammi stood defiantly, her cape flowing in the breeze. "*Ha!* Your time is up, granny!" AeroStar said, adjusting the slightly oversize tiara on her eleven-year-old head. "*This is my time now.*"

"Funny thing you'll learn about jumping through wormholes," Sammi said. "It can get confusing if you don't have friends to remind you which side you belong on."

"Then it seems we have something else in common—I never had any friends, and you'll never see yours again."

Sammi crouched into her best jiujitsu attack position. "That's why I came back. To remind you that you didn't just pick the wrong world to take over—*you picked the wrong body.*"

Sammi leaped into the air, diving straight at AeroStar, who quickly tried to blast her with her tiara. The oversize tiara kicked back, wobbling as it shot. Sammi was able to dodge the errant blast and regrouped as AeroStar readjusted her deadly headgear. She took the opening to dive again and tackled AeroStar to the ground. The two of them rolled across the gravelly rooftop until AeroStar was able to get her legs under Sammi. She flung the elderly-bodied Sammi off in the air, and Sammi landed hard on the edge of the roof. Before she could get her wind back and scramble to her feet, AeroStar pounced. She pinned Sammi down, holding her head and upper body dangerously over the edge. AeroStar laughed as she looked down, past Sammi, at the citizens of Merwinsville still fighting the Audreenian Non-Carnivorous Giant Podling Plants.

"You're as pathetic as the rest of your town down there," she snarled. "Thinking you can *actually* be a hero. Let me tell *you* something *I've* learned—" She flipped Sammi around, letting her fall for a second, then grabbed her cape at the last second. Sammi was suspended over the ledge with AeroStar the only thing keeping her from falling to the street below. AeroStar leaned out and whispered in Sammi's ear, "There are no *real heroes*."

"*HOLD IT RIGHT THERE!*" AeroStar turned her head, shocked to see GOR-DON standing on the top of the rooftop stairwell, holding three silver N.E.D. suits in his hands. "Don't make me use these," he said threateningly.

"Wh—what are you doing here?" AeroStar said, still holding Sammi over the edge of the building. "*I ordered you to destroy those! You work for me, remember?*"

The G'Dalien shrugged. "I was thinking of taking some time off." He smirked at Sammi, who was watching from her precarious perch. "I believe it's called a *vacation.* Thought I might travel through the wormhole, maybe bring back a couple of AlienSlayers, see what they think of what's going on around here."

Even in her horribly dangerous position, Sammi smiled proudly at this. AeroStar narrowed her glare. "All right," she spat. *"What do you want?"*

GOR-DON stepped over to the open vent, which was still burning meat below. He held the suits over the chute that dropped directly into the red-hot brick oven. "Let her go, and I'll burn these right here, right now."

"GOR-DON, *no!*" Sammi screamed. "It doesn't matter what happens to me! Take the suits and save Alex and Herbert! *Please!*"

AeroStar looked from GOR-DON, standing with the suits over the open flame, to Sammi, who was near tears. She grinned back at the G'Dalien. *"Deal."*

She yanked Sammi back onto the rooftop and pushed her down onto the gravel. Sammi rolled and scrambled toward GOR-DON, just as he dropped the N.E.D. suits into the vent. "*No!*" she screamed again. She ran to the chute and looked. The flames devoured the suits in seconds. A gust of hot, silvery ash blew out of the vent and all around her. Sammi slid down to a slump. GOR-DON approached to help her up.

GET AWAY FROM ME.

An evil chuckle of delight came from the edge of the roof. They both looked over. AeroStar was enjoying this misery. "Well, now, what have we learned?" she said coyly. "As I was saying, there are no real heroes. Sure, this fat, disobedient blob might have saved your miserable life, but he also sealed the fates of your friends, making you hate him." She grinned broadly up at GOR-DON. "And you, throwing away your moment to shine as well as any chance of *ever* seeing that ridiculous lunch lady you're so fond of. This is too delicious! I knew my Three-and-a-Half-Point Plan of Vengeance was perfect, but I never expected it to be *this much fun!*"

CRUNCH! The building suddenly shook as if it were being knocked down by a MagnaWrecker. AeroStar teetered near the edge and looked down. The Audreenian Non-Carnivorous Giant Podling Plants had broken through the Merwinsvillian citizens'

valiant but unsuccessful front and were now steadily scaling the building, honing in on the source of those sweet, spicy, smoky smells of baking meat.

CRUNCH! One of them reared its head back and slammed it into the upper wall again, taking a giant bite out of the brick, then spitting the chunk out in disgust. AeroStar stumbled back, away from the edge, but her tiara fell down around her eyes, blinding her to the sight of the first of the plant monsters reaching the top of the building. She fumbled with her golden head-weapon, trying to straighten it to blast the creatures. Doing this, she knocked it up and off her head. The golden weapon bounced twice off the gravel, rolled along the ledge, and tumbled over the side.

"*Aaaaaauugh!*" The first of the pod-creatures lifted its root-foot over the edge and stood up, towering over AeroStar. She scrambled toward the center of the roof and ducked behind GOR-DON. "I command you to save me! *I am your Queen!*"

GOR-DON grinned and pretended to be confused. "Wait. *Sammi? Is that you? This is too confusing. Gosh, I guess I'm such a moron, I don't understand!*"

The real Sammi stood up and crouched again to take on the creatures. She leaped toward the first pod-monster—*THWACK!*—and was smacked away by its sail-sized leaf-appendage, sending her crashing into the vent. The other three pod-monsters had reached the top of the building, and they were all inhaling deeply through their olfactory pores. With each deep breath of the meat-filled air, they became more aggressive—and more hungry. Thick ribbons of plant drool oozed from their snapping mouths as they descended upon GOR-DON, the juiciest-looking morsel on the roof.

Sammi shook off her setback and dived onto the lead plant's root-foot. It kicked and roared as she scrambled up the beast, scaling its stalk. The plant writhed and twisted, trying to buck her off so it could get to its G'Dalien sushi snack below.

As GOR-DON ran in circles trying to dodge the snapping jaws of two other alien pod-monsters, the cowering AeroStar crawled toward the stairwell. She was about to escape when the last pod-monster leaped into the air and landed with a *CRASH!*—directly between her and her escape route. "*I just wanna go home,*" she whimpered.

Over the roars and noise and snapping jaws, a louder sound suddenly grew from the street below: the sound of the citizens of Merwinsville, *cheering.* Sammi stopped yanking on her pod-plant's root hairs and leaped off its back. She looked over to the edge of the building. She heard a blast, and more cheering, and then saw to her amazement a figure rise in midair and into view.

It was Old Man Alex. He had his El Solo Libre costume on: Mexican wrestling mask, poorly crafted towel-cape, and ill-fitting tighty-whities—over a N.E.D. suit. And he'd added something else to his getup: AeroStar's golden tiara fit his adult head better than hers, and the mini jetpacks

jutting out of it were suspending him above the cheering crowd. Extending from his tiara were a pair of mechanical arms, which had a firm grip on Herbert and Alex. They too were wearing the *real* N.E.D. suits.

Sammi looked over at GOR-DON, who'd stopped running in circles just long enough to see this spectacle. He met Sammi's gaze and shrugged as he smiled at her.

"So what were those?" Sammi shouted, nodding toward the oven vent.

"Something I found in Herbert's garbage bin," GOR-DON said. "Amazing what you humans will throw away."

"AlienSlayers!" Old Man Alex shouted so that everyone below could hear him. "Time to exterminate these dillweeds!" He set down his two sidekicks, and they rolled off in different directions. The mechanical arms shot back into his tiara and were replaced with a blaster. He aimed it at the pod-monster near Sammi and— *FRRZZZZAAATTT!* With a quick blast, the alien plant was instantly blown to smithereens. The

entire roof was showered with green, goopy herbaplasmic goo. Herbert and Alex were already halfway across the rooftop, leaping into action to rescue GOR-DON. They slid baseball-style straight at the two pod-creatures terrorizing him, grabbing handfuls of gravel as they slammed into the pod-monsters' feet. When the two aliens stumbled and looked down, Herbert and Alex whipped gravel up at their snapping, budlike heads. They roared and began trying to stomp on these pests, who twisted and dodged their attempts until the two weed creatures' stems were completely entangled. They fell to the ground with a *CRASH!*—writhing like a pair of twisted snakes, offering an easy shot for Old Man Alex.

FRRZZZZAAATTT! In the next second, another downpour of green goop rained over everyone.

The last Audreenian Non-Carnivorous Giant Podling Plant moved from its position blocking the stairwell and charged at Herbert and Alex. As it did, AeroStar took the opportunity to sneak down the stairs. She burst out into the crowd gathered in front of the building and ran immediately into her hugest fans, Moose and Adriana. *"There she is!"* Adriana cried, hugging her. "Thank goodness you're safe! Wait, why aren't you up there saving the day?"

"Never mind that now," Moose added. "I'm sure she has her reasons. What she needs is a good superhero name. We came up with some great ones." Moose pulled a crumpled piece of paper out of his pocket. "'SuperSammi'... uh, 'SammiSlayer.' Ooh—you'll love this one. Ready? *'THE SLAMMIN' SAMINATOR!'*"

Four stories above them, the plant creature charged Alex and Herbert. They waited until the last second then dived out of the way. The creature's spindly root-feet slipped on the slimy plant goo covering the roof and slid straight toward the ledge. As it careened over the side, Old Man Alex looked down at the tightly gathered crowd below. Seeing they were in danger of being crushed, he dived off the roof like a cliff diver and aimed his tiara blaster at the plummeting plant beast.

FZZZZZAAAATT!

Directly below, Moose and Adriana were still holding AeroStar hostage when they were suddenly drenched in bright green Audreenian Non-Carnivorous Giant Podling Plant goo. They wiped their eyes in time to join the rest of the crowd as they looked up and saw Old Man Alex hovering over them by way of his tiara jetpack. He zoomed over them as they burst out into cheers of *"LEE-BRAY! LEE-BRAY! LEE-BRAY!"* Old Man Alex soaked up the praise before flying to the edge of Andretti's rooftop, where he took his place beside his partners, Herbert and Alex. Sammi stepped behind them and gave them all a giant hug. With a look of confusion, the three of them glanced at the 111-year-old supposed archenemy .

"I'll explain later," Sammi said.

"No need, *dudette*," said the person who looked like Alex but spoke an awful lot like Old Man Alex. "We're down with the whole switcheroo! Like, *really down*."

Sammi blinked in disbelief. She looked at the person she thought was Old Man Alex. "We get it," he said, exactly the way Alex would. "Pretty *awesome*, right?" The two Alexes chuckled to each other and high-fived.

CHAPTER 41

The *Fluffy Stuff 'n' Pals Teaparty Townhouse* was at full capacity, more crowded than it had ever been, and Ellie, scurrying around serving everyone tea, had never been happier. In addition to the hundreds of stuffed animals, crammed together upstairs were Alex (in Old Man Alex's body), Old Man Alex (in Alex's body), Sammi (in AeroStar's body), AeroStar (in Sammi's body), and GOR-DON and Herbert (in their own bodies, thankfully).

Alex and Old Man Alex's exciting account about their adventure rescuing the G'Daliens, including how the rebuilding of Future Merwinsville was under way, left Sammi grinning from ear to wrinkly, 111-year-old ear.

"Nice bit of heroing there, Los Duo Libres," Sammi said, tapping the ornate weapon still on the older Alex's head. "And you did all of that without any jet-pack popping, blaster-equipped golden tiaras."

"Thanks," Alex said. "But please—we prefer Golden Crown of Awesomeness."

She looked at them both. "Are you sure you two . . . *got switched?*"

"Yep, sure did!" Alex replied.

"I know. Pretty funky, huh?" Old Man Alex asked. "Kinda mind-blowing when you look at us." He made a little explosion motion with his hand against his brain.

"Actually, it's kind of hard to tell any difference at all. No offense."

Alex and Old Man Alex stared at each other for a moment then broke into wide grins. "*Awesome!*" they both said. Old Man Alex high-fived Alex then walked over to bug Herbert, who was tinkering with his N.E.D. suit.

Alex looked Sammi's 111-year-old body up and down as she stuffed herself into a N.E.D. suit. "So, what's it like being—*in her body?*"

"I told you it'd be weird meeting my future self," she said. "But this is kind of ridiculous." She glanced over at AeroStar, sulking in the corner, wearing the third N.E.D. suit and hugging a stuffed mongoose. "Going through again better undo this."

"I dunno. It wouldn't be so bad if it didn't," Alex said. "Make for a great school picture this year. Bet we'd win 'Most Matured Since Last Year.'"

Sammi punched Alex in the arm. He burst out laughing.

GOR-DON slithered over to AeroStar in the corner, awkwardly squeezing himself in next to her and a rather large plush hippopotamus. "If you came here to gloat and make me feel bad, don't

bother," she said without looking up. "My Three-and-a-Half-Point Plan of Vengeance was a complete failure. I couldn't feel any worse."

"I just thought I'd say good-bye," GOR-DON said. "I probably won't see you again after you go back through."

"You're staying *here?*" she asked coldly.

"Yeah. My one-point plan is to curl up and die in a garbage Dumpster."

"Technically that's two points. But hey, congratulations. You're more pathetic than me."

He got up to leave, then turned to face her again. "Little advice from one friendless jerk to another: *you can change* if you really want to."

AeroStar looked up as he began to slither away. "I had friends once, y'know!"

Everyone stopped talking and turned toward AeroStar. Sammi stepped closer, and AeroStar looked up at her. "You said before I didn't have any friends; that's what was different. *It's not true.* I had exactly one day, when I was your age, when I had two friends. I didn't want to go to my swim meet, so I ran into my neighbor's yard, and hid in the tube slide in his jungle gym." She looked at Old

Man Alex. "You two had these silver suits on, and you saw me and you took them off. I think you were embarrassed."

Old Man Alex shrugged. "I might've had a teensy crush on you."

Sammi and Alex shared a glance.

"So what'd you do?" Sammi said quickly.

"I stayed. I stayed and we played. And it was— *the most fun I'd ever had.* We made up rhyming food names for each other. I was Hammy Sammi. The weird, brainy kid was Herbert Sherbet. And you were . . . uh—"

"Alex Shallots," Old Man Alex said. "It's a hard one to remember because it doesn't really rhyme. But I always liked it."

"But why just the one day?" Alex asked. "Why didn't you stay friends?"

"I made a choice. I decided I had to do more important things, and I didn't have time for silly nicknames. I made up my mind that friends would get in the way, slow me down, keep me from becoming successful."

"Wow," Alex said. "That's really . . . *stupid.*"

"Thanks. I kinda know that now," she said softly.

"Well," Sammi said, "I know a couple of guys who are pretty good dudes. About your age, too. Or at least they will be when we all go through that wormhole and get back into our proper bodies. I have a feeling you three might have a lot in common, even if it's one day a long, long time ago."

AeroStar stood up and looked curiously at Sammi, who was smiling at her. "It's strange, looking at my own face with you in it," AeroStar said. "I can't remember the last time I saw myself smile like that."

"Well, you'll have your face back in a minute, I hope," said Sammi. "Then you can do whatever you want with it. But I highly recommend smiling."

They shared a smile, and Sammi turned to the others. "Okay, gang. You all know the plan. She and I will go through first. Then we'll send our suits through for the rest of you to come join us. Herbert, you coming with us or waiting?"

"I'll take the next car," Herbert said. "I don't want to risk some sort of Sammi-Aero-Herbert-Star hybrid experiment. I look horrible in tights."

Sammi nodded, then hit the switches on the suits. The wormhole fired up, and the two of them felt the warm tug toward it. Before they leaped, AeroStar glanced back at GOR-DON, sulking in the same spot where she'd been sitting.

FLOOMPH!

CHAPTER 42

POP! POP! Sammi and AeroStar flew out of the wormhole and tumbled onto the sandy floor of the caveman diorama. All was quiet and empty. Sammi stood up first, opened her eyes widely, and looked down at herself. "Hey! *I'm me again!*"

AeroStar got up slowly. "Yeah. Me, too."

They removed their suits and shot them back through the wormhole. A minute later, Alex and Old Man Alex popped out and rolled onto the floor. They stood up and looked at each other, then burst into giggles. "*Awesome!*" They high-fived again.

"I can't tell—did they switch back, too?" Sammi asked.

"Does it matter?" Sammi said.

POP! Herbert was the last to come flying out of the wormhole. Reunited, they all walked out into the Hallway of Human History and made their way to the abandoned museum lobby. Together they pushed open the great door, then stepped into the sunshine and gazed out over the city.

"I don't believe it," AeroStar said.

"Whoa," Sammi said.

Laid out before them was the city of Merwinsville, already well on its way to becoming better than ever. Built along the banks of the massive clearing the S.S. *Clemtanic* had created were the beginnings of a whole new city. The

G'Daliens had gone to work right away.

"Wow," Alex said. "Those G'Daliens are good."

"No," Herbert said. "They're geniuses."

"Try playing tic-tac-toe with one sometime," Old Man Alex said.

A familiar voice came calling from the bottom of the museum steps. "Not a bad start, eh, Herbie?" Old Man Herbert floated up on his airchair then stopped short at the sight of AeroStar standing with his friends. He hit the console on his armrest

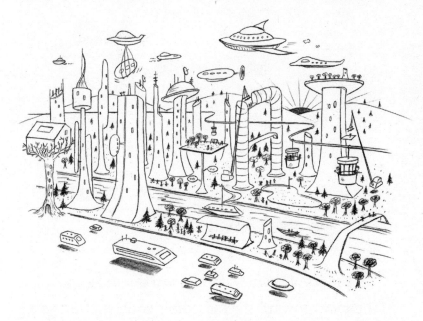

and a giant laser blaster popped out of the back of his chair, taking direct aim on the old woman's forehead. "Someone tell me what's going on, please."

"Relax," Herbert assured his 111-year-old self. "It's all right."

"B-but, it's *AeroStar*—"

She stepped forward and smiled. She reached up and took off her cape. "Please. Call me . . . *Hammy Sammi.*"

The six of them walked down the steps and made their way toward the incredible construction going on all around them. The G'Daliens made the work fun and effortless, like a massive neighborhood block party. They soon found Chicago, Dallas, Sausalito, Mr. Illinois, and EL-ROY and joined them in helping to rebuild their city. For Alex, Herbert, and Sammi, it was a perfect way to spend one last perfect day, together in Future Merwinsville.

As the sun set over the newly constructed towers of downtown, Alex, Sammi, and Herbert finally said their good-byes to their G'Dalien and human friends. They gave their elder selves big hugs and promised to stay in touch by use of the Parallel Universe Perspective Enhancers. They parted ways near the partying construction site, and as the ex-AlienSlayers looked back, they smiled at the sight of their 111-year-old selves making their way into the crowd, as friends.

Alex, Herbert, and Sammi walked back toward

the Museum of Human History, each of them wondering silently what they should do with the N.E.D. suits.

"We can't destroy them," Alex finally blurted out. "We all know how Herbert's whole solemn vow of silence thing worked out last time."

"I still feel they could threaten the delicate balance of the time-space continuum," Herbert said. "Especially in the wrong hands. We learned *that*, too."

"You're both right," Sammi said after some consideration. "And I think the answer is simple. We just need to figure out a way to somehow use them for good."

"Like what?" Alex wondered aloud.

"*Wait! Wait! HOLD UP, Y'ALL!*"

A voice called after them. They turned to see Marion running toward them. She was winded when she finally caught up to them. "I'm so glad I didn't miss you. I just wanted to say thank you for the rip-roaring adventure, and, well, *adios amigos*."

"Thank *you*," Herbert said. "We couldn't have done any of this without you and that wonderful pet of yours. Please give Mr. Nibbles a big belly scratch for me."

Alex and Sammi stared at Herbert in disbelief.

Marion grinned at them oddly for a few awkward seconds. Her cheeks grew two or three deeper shades of pink, and she began to giggle uncontrollably.

"Marion?" Sammi asked. "Are you all right?"

"Well, there is *one other thing*," she said, trying to pull herself together. "I heard ol' *Gordo* has been staying back with you. How, uh—*how's he doing?*"

"Horrible," said Alex. "He's a miserable piece of—"

"He's *terrific*," Herbert lied. "Really loving life, putting himself out there. You know ol' *Gordo*. Can't keep a G'Dalien like that down, no sir."

"Oh. Er, well, that's great," Marion said. "I just—uh, please just tell him Marion says hello. A lady can get to doing a lot of thinking up there on the dark side of the moon when it's just her and a Klapthorian Death Slug, and, well, I guess sometimes my mind would wander back to when he and I were, uh . . ."

She smiled at some memory, then quickly snapped out of it. "*Ahem.* Yes, well—just please tell him I said, 'We'll always have Meatloaf Mondays.'"

She turned abruptly and began to walk quickly back toward the crowd. Alex looked at Herbert. "What was *that*? And why'd you tell her he was doing *terrific*?"

"You clearly know nothing about girls," Herbert said. "Evolutionary mating data shows that females are disinterested in males in a damaged or wounded state."

"You mean, like, balled up in the corner of a *Fluffy Stuff 'n' Pals Teaparty Townhouse*, rocking back and forth with a roomful of stuffed animals?"

"Precisely."

Sammi rolled her eyes. "You're both wrong about girls. What we really like is to be *romanced*. Candles, music, a nice dinn—" She stopped suddenly. *"That's it!"* she shouted. "Wait here!"

Sammi ran over to catch up to Marion. Herbert and Alex couldn't hear what she was saying, but it made Marion giggle loudly, jump up and down happily, and give Sammi a ginormous hug. After a few more minutes of intimate discussion, Sammi ran back to the boys.

"Shall we?" she said, heading toward the museum steps.

ONE WEEK LATER
(AND 100 YEARS EARLIER)

Alex, Herbert, and Sammi walked along the side of Herbert's house to the large garbage bin. They held their noses and knocked.

"*NOBODY HOME. GO AWAY,*" a muffled voice said from inside. Alex rolled his eyes and opened the bin. The three of them looked down at GOR-DON, lying in a clump on a blanket of discarded silver suits, staring up at them. Littered around him were empty chocolate pudding cups.

"Hey, big fella," Herbert said. "You busy?"

"Swamped," GOR-DON said.

"We thought you might need some cheering up, so we got you a little gift," Sammi said.

GOR-DON looked up at them. Sammi handed him a large box wrapped in bright pink paper. "Is this some kind of trick? A self-detonating proton neutralizer or something?"

"That *would* be hilarious," Herbert said. "But it's just a gift."

GOR-DON sat up and violently clawed at the box, ripping it to shreds. He looked confused as he lifted out what was inside: a perfectly tailored G'Dalien tuxedo. *In silver.*

"What is the meaning of this?" he spat, looking at them.

"It's just part one of a *two-and-a-half-point surprise* we have for you," Sammi said. "But you have to trust us."

"*Pff*," GOR-DON snorted. "Why on Grebular would I do that?"

"Uh, because you've been living in my trash bin for about a week," Herbert said.

"And in my sister's dollhouse for about a month before that," Alex added. "And we could've told everyone and become rich and famous for giving to the world a real, live, super-bummed-out alien, but we haven't. *Yet.*"

"Just try it on," Sammi said. "I bet you'll look *so* handsome in it."

GOR-DON's nose-hole twitched as he eyed his three ex-archenemies. He held the silver tux up in front of him. "It smells a little like cheese," he sneered. "Which pleases me greatly." He held the multiarmed tuxedo in front of him. "Okay. Now you three turn around. I'm a little shy. *TURN!*"

They smiled as they did what he asked. When they turned back, they were pleasantly surprised. GOR-DON stood before them in an all-silver, perfectly fitting tuxedo.

"Dude, you look *cool!*" Alex said.

"Well, I don't know about *cool*," GOR-DON said, hiding a grin and looking down at himself. "Sammi, what do you think?"

She stepped forward and took his hands in hers, looking him up and down. "I think," she said quietly, "that you're ready for the second part of your two-and-a-half-point surprise."

They led a blindfolded GOR-DON into Alex's yard and up the stairs of the tea party town house, with a blindfold over his beady black eyes. "I swear, if this is some sort of trick, I'm gonna slaughter you guys," the dapperly dressed G'Dalien said good-naturedly.

They stood him in the middle of the upstairs room and removed his blindfold. His grin sank as he looked down and saw the tiny tea party table set for two, with the fat, stuffed hippopotamus seated across from one empty chair.

"Surprise!" Alex said. "It's a blind date!"

GOR-DON stared at the hippo, then spun around and snapped on them. *"YOU EVIL VERMIN! YOU KNOW I'M STRUGGLING WITH SELF-WORTH ISSUES! HOW DARE YOU DECEIVE ME INTO THINKING I MIGHT HAVE A CHANCE AT HAPPINESS AGAIN WHEN YOU KNOW HOW VULNERABLE I AM! I*

SHOULD RIP OUT YOUR HEARTS AND CRUSH THEM WITH MY . . . my . . ." He broke down sobbing.

"Jeez," Alex said. *"Calm down."*

"Gosh," Herbert added.

Sammi stepped up to GOR-DON and gave him a big hug. "Silly G'Dalien," she said. "This isn't your blind date—"

She flicked a switch on the back of his tuxedo. "This is." He looked down at himself as the silver tuxedo blinked and flashed to life, its insides humming and buzzing. He spun around to see the fake decal mirror on the wall suddenly turn a swirly electric blue. The wormhole pulled at him as the entire town house began to tremble.

WUBBA-WUBBA-WUBBA-WUBBA-WUBBA! He had panic in his eyes as he grabbed at anything near him—tables, chairs, the hippo—but nothing could stop his inevitable swallowing as the wormhole grew stronger and sucked him in.

"NO!" He cried out, *"I'LL DESTROY YOU FOR THIS!"*

Alex, Herbert, and Sammi stood back and smiled, waving good-bye to their G'Dalien friend.

POOMPH!

WUBBA WUBBA WUBBA

NOOOO!!!

The three of them looked at one another. "Who's up for Andretti's pizza?" Alex asked. They walked down the stairs together, out of the tea party town house and into the warm sunshine of Present Day Merwinsville.

PLOP!

GOR-DON shot out of the wormhole in a blob, his beautiful silver tuxedo a bit wrinkled from the journey, but still quite spiffy. He stood up to find himself in the dimly lit caveman diorama. He glanced around in a panic and froze when he heard the chilling sound of a woman's voice from the black void.

"It's about time. *I was wondering when I'd see you again.*"

GOR-DON dropped to his knees and blubbered

like a giant baby. "Oh, *pleeeeze, pleeeeze forgive me, AeroStar, your Worshipfulness! I never meant to betray you! It was those AlienSlayers again! They tricked me! They kidnapped me and made me hide out! I was actually spying on them for you, my queen!*"

There was silence for a moment. Then a match lit. GOR-DON slowly stood, trying to fixate on the tiny source of light. It lit a candle, then another. Either curious or resigned to his fate, he stepped toward what looked like a small table holding two candles in the center of the caveman diorama.

"You can call me queen if you like," the voice said in a kinder tone. "So long as you promise to always be my king."

As he approached, the lights came up very slightly, revealing a scene he never could have expected. Seated there at a romantically set table for two was Marion, dressed in a beautiful gown. There were two Mega-Choco-Bomb Root Beer Marshmallow Smoothies and a fresh, hot Andretti's pizza. GOR-DON looked around and saw the cave mannequins dressed like fancy waiters, and he saw that the light source was from twinkly lights tastefully strewn on the now-upright stuffed woolly mammoth.

As he walked past his chair and knelt down at Marion's side, GOR-DON felt as if he were in a dream. He gently took her hand and kissed it. Then he stood up without saying a word and invited her to do the same. She grinned, trying not to giggle as she stood and let him take her in his tentacles.

GOR-DON smiled as he and Marion swayed back and forth together as they danced under the watchful gaze of the stuffed woolly mammoth.

THE END